"Just take off my sister's wedding dress!"

MacKenzie Grier's voice was tight as he spoke through clenched teeth.

"With pleasure," Cinnamon said. She turned and headed for the stairs, holding up the hem of the dress and mindful of her bare feet. She knew trying on the gown was something she should not have done, but it was so beautiful, she couldn't resist. She should have just called the dress shop and explained there had been a mistake. Once in her room, she tried to undo the buttons on the dress, but got nowhere. She tried everything, but nothing worked.

"What's taking so long?" he bellowed up the stairs.

"I can't get the buttons undone," she shouted back.

"I'll help." A second later, he stood in the bedroom doorway.

"What are you doing here?" she asked. For one charged moment, they stared at each other.

"Look, do you want my help or not? One way or another, you're getting out of that dress!"

Books by Shirley Hailstock

Kimani Romance

My Lover, My Friend
Wrong Dress, Right Guy

Silhouette Special Edition

A Father's Fortune
Love on Call

SHIRLEY HAILSTOCK

began her writing life as a lover of reading. She liked nothing better than to find a corner in the library and get lost in a book, explore new worlds and visit places she never expected to see. As an author, not only can she visit those places, but she can be the heroine of her own stories.

A past president of Romance Writers of America, Shirley holds a Waldenbooks Award for bestselling romance and a Career Achievement Award from *Romantic Times BOOKreviews*. She is the recipient of an Emma Merritt Award for service to RWA and a Lifetime Achievement Award from the New York City chapter. Contact Shirley at shirley.hailstock@comcast.net or visit her Web site at www.geocities.com/shailstock.

Wrong DRESS, Right GUY

SHIRLEY HAILSTOCK

KIMANI
ROMANCE

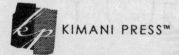

KIMANI PRESS™

ISBN-13: 978-0-373-86070-8
ISBN-10:   0-373-86070-6

WRONG DRESS, RIGHT GUY

www.kimanipress.com

Printed in U.S.A.

Dear Reader,

Don't you just love weddings?

Like Cinnamon Scott in *Wrong Dress, Right Guy,* I love all the trappings of the day: the planning, the fights between families, not to mention the bridesmaids, the smiles and the tears on everyone's faces. I love the flowers and the quiet somberness of the sanctuary or temple. But mostly I love the wedding gowns. Having once worked in a bridal shop and been a bridal model, the dress does it for me. There's something about putting on that white lace that makes you want to dance in the beauty and strength of strong arms.

And the groom and his men—all those hunky guys, dressed to the nines and escorting the bridesmaids— they're part of the day, too. MacKenzie Grier is just such a man, however, his own experience with nuptials has soured him on anything to do with weddings and marriage. Then he meets Cinnamon, a woman who turns his life upside down each time she walks in the room. Seeing her in a wedding gown turns out to be more than a fantasy.

I enjoyed meeting and learning about Cinnamon and Mac. I hope you enjoy your time with them, too.

Sincerely yours,

Shirley Hailstock

To my mother, who inspires me every day.

Chapter 1

She knew it was wrong.

Even as she stepped into the center of the cloud of fabric and pulled the dress up over her body, Cinnamon Scott knew she shouldn't do it. But the wedding gown was just too beautiful not to try on. Too irresistible. Pulling the gown up, she buttoned the long line of buttons that adorned the back of the dress. Looking in the long mirror in her bedroom, she gasped at her image. That couldn't be *her.*

A bride.

The image stared back at her. White lace with flowers. The neckline was scooped and the sleeves extended to her fingers. She turned all the way around, staring at herself, admiring the dress and how it made her feel. She felt more than excitement. The dress symbolized promises, vows and the glow of love.

Then the doorbell rang. Cinnamon jumped, startled by the sound. Her stomach dropped as if she'd just plunged down a steep roller coaster.

The delivery man was back!

Her hands went to steady her stomach. Before the sound finished reverberating through the house, she was already reaching for the buttons on the back of the dress. Fumbling to undo the small pearl orbs, her fingers kept sliding off them. The bell rang again, this time the man punched it several times, causing the sound to start and stop as if it were hiccupping. Cinnamon worked the twenty-two inches of buttons as fast as she could, but they were insistent on remaining within their minuscule loops.

On the bride's wedding night, these might be fun for the groom to undo one at a time as he kissed his way to her skin, but at this moment she wished they would just open the way a normal button would.

"Damn." Cinnamon cursed as the stuttering bell sounded again. Thirty seconds and three rings later, she gave up. Hiking the skirt up above her bare feet, she headed for the stairs. Her feet made rapid whispering sounds as she ran. The bell continued to ring.

What was wrong with the guy? she thought. Anger ripped through her. He had her so rattled, she nearly yanked the door off its hinges.

There was a man there, but not the young delivery guy who had dropped off the wrong dress.

This man had his back to her. The delivery guy had been muscular, wearing jeans and a golf shirt with the bridal shop logo on his breast pocket. This man wore jeans and a short-sleeved shirt. He was tall with short hair and a posture that said either FBI or military personnel. *Drill sergeant* flew into her mind. What did he want? He couldn't be here about the dress; why would anyone send the FBI for a wedding gown?

Cinnamon mentally shook herself. What was wrong with her? A TV weather girl from Boston shouldn't be thinking military or FBI just because she was now located within a breath of the District of Columbia.

"May I help you?" she asked the man's broad back.

Her words and the man turning were simultaneous. His hand had begun its arcing movement, poised and ready to accost the bell for another set of rings. He stopped, staring at her. His gaze seemed to envelop her.

He was definitely *not* the delivery man. That man had had a welcoming smile on his face as he presented her with a dress bag from Amanda's Bridal and Tuxedo Shoppe. She'd returned his smile. Accepting the dress bag, she'd run up the winding staircase. Her dress had finally arrived! She'd ordered the gown almost as soon as she'd discovered the shop. She'd come down from Boston and loved the beautiful quiet village the moment she'd seen it. It wasn't the same as she remembered from her childhood.

The alterations were complete and Cinnamon felt like a teenager preparing for her first party, even though the ball was a full month away.

Mary Ellen Taylor, a friend from college, was giving her annual Start of the Summer Ball and Cinnamon had promised to return to Boston for it. Moreover, Wesley Garner had asked her to go with him and she wouldn't give up the chance to hang on his arm. Eye candy didn't even come close to describing how gorgeous he was.

This man wasn't as physically good-looking as Wesley, but he still stopped her heart. Then she saw the anger in his eyes as they came level with hers. His mouth opened, but the moment he noticed the dress, he stopped. He looked her up and down as if she'd robbed him of the ability to speak English. His face went from a normal shade of brown to a dark raging red. Cinnamon stepped back to get out of the way of the heated fury she saw there. Without invitation, he opened the screened door and stepped inside.

"You have got some nerve," he said. "What were you thinking?"

"I beg your pardon?" Cinnamon said.

"That is not your dress." He pointed toward her. How did he know that?

"What gives you the right to put on someone else's wedding gown?" he continued.

She looked down at herself. It was then she noticed the white dress bag over his arm, the bridal shop logo clearly visible on a square of clear plastic. This bag was identical to the one lying open on her bed upstairs.

"*This* is your dress." He dropped the bag on the sofa.

"I'm sorry," she said, inadequately. "It's so beautiful." Cinnamon ran her hands on the delicate fabric. "Before I knew what I was doing, I had it on." She looked down at the dress again.

It was truly the most beautiful dress she'd ever

seen. It was beautifully jeweled with tiny pearls and lacy flowers delicate enough for a queen. She remembered her image in the full-length mirror in the bedroom. She'd never felt so...she could hardly think of the word—*happy.* Tears misted her eyes as she saw herself as a bride.

"You must be the worst kind of airhead."

The man's words snapped her back to the present. "Excuse me," she said, making no attempt to keep her voice low or to hide the anger in it. "Who the hell are you, anyway?"

"MacKenzie Grier," he stated as if she should recognize his name.

Cinnamon raised an eyebrow.

"Brother of Allison Grier," he continued.

"And she would be..."

"The *bride.*"

"Oh" was all Cinnamon could say. "I'm sorry, I haven't met her. I've only actually been in the house a short while. I wondered who the gown belonged to."

"Does that make it better? If you don't know the bride, is it easier to wear her clothes?"

"I said I was sorry. What do you want, blood? It's not like I've ruined it or anything. And don't go saying anything about bad luck because that's a crock and I'm sure you know it."

If his face could get any darker, Cinnamon would be surprised. She knew trying on the dress wasn't something she should have done, but his reaction was totally over-the-top.

"Just take the dress off so I can get out of here." His voice was tight, and he spoke through clenched teeth.

"With pleasure," Cinnamon said, directing a hard stare at him. It was lost, she thought, on the equally hard look he leveled in her direction.

She turned and headed for the stairs, holding the dress up and mindful of her bare feet. His eyes bored into her. She felt the weight of his stare and remembered the dress wasn't totally closed at the back. A wave of heat went through her and she caught herself before tripping on the stairs.

In her room she tried to open the buttons, but got nowhere. The more she worked the length of buttons, the shorter her arms seemed to get. A full ten minutes had gone by when she heard his voice from below stairs. "What's taking so long?"

"I can't get the buttons open," she shouted back.

"I'll help." She whirled around a moment later as the sound of his voice was much closer. He stood in her bedroom doorway. Her hands hung in the air as if she were practicing to be a contortionist. Stepping back, she nearly tripped over her feet.

"What are you doing here?" she asked. It was a stupid question. She heard herself right after the words left her mouth. He hadn't been in the door when he'd shouted that she was taking a long time. So he had to have come up the steps after she answered.

"Look, do you want my help or not? One way or another you're getting out of that dress."

For a charged moment they stared at each other. Neither moved nor said a word. "I know how I came on downstairs," he finally said. "But I assure you I am not a rapist. I only want my sister's dress."

"And I have only your word for that."

"You tried on the dress to see what you'd look like in it—and I have only your word for that."

Somehow one didn't have anything to do with the other. Cinnamon knew the ball was in her court. He had not moved from the doorway and appeared to have no intention of stepping across the threshold without an invitation. After a long moment she pushed herself toward him.

Cinnamon couldn't put her feelings in perspective. MacKenzie unnerved her, but she felt more was going on than that. She felt some invisible tension between them; she wouldn't say *connecting* them. But it was there and it made no sense.

She didn't know him, had never laid eyes on him until a few minutes ago, yet he was somehow familiar and she knew his hands would be hot and electric if they touched her. When she was close enough to him she turned around.

And held her breath.

"At least tell me your name," he said. "I should know whose body I'm about to put my hands on." Heat flashed through her like an exploding volcano. It wouldn't surprise Cinnamon if she looked down and found the fire inside her had changed the gown's color from white to crimson-red.

"Cinnamon Scott." She gave him her name.

"You're Zahara Lewis's—"

"Granddaughter," she finished for him.

"I'm sorry about her passing. I really liked her. She was very kind to me."

He touched her skin and Cinnamon jumped. "Thank you," she said, trying to cover her reaction. She swallowed hard to get her voice back. "I didn't know you knew her." She felt his hands. They were large and sure and warm against the exposed skin of her back. He leaned down to look at the buttons and she felt his breath on her neck. Her eyes closed and she wanted to lean into him, feel the sensations that rioted through her when his breath caressed her skin. She wanted to savor the warmth of it, inhale its sensual scent. Just in time, she caught herself, snapping her eyes wide open and forcing herself to remember where she was.

Cinnamon didn't understand her reaction. She concentrated on her breathing to take her mind off the feel of his hands. Her breasts grew heavy and she put her hands up to keep the dress from falling off her shoulders. It seemed to take him an eon to finish the buttons.

"Everyone knew Zahara. She was a pillar in this community," he was saying when her mind returned to her surroundings.

"I know. I have some letters from her." Cinnamon had only read the letters recently. Her grandmother's words prompted her to refuse an offer to sell the house and made Cinnamon decide to move into the house herself. Securing a job at the National Weather Service capped the decision.

"Why didn't you ever visit her? She has pictures of you, but only as a little girl. I don't remember ever seeing you here or her saying you'd been here."

Cinnamon wasn't about to get into the mother/father issues that went on in her family. "Time, career, things you believe are important keep you busy," she said. "Then one day it's too late to do anything about it." She hadn't intended to say that. His hands had already generated heat in her and obviously they were melting her mind.

"What career are you in?"

"I reported the weather at a television station in Boston," she said, refusing to use the term weather girl. "But I chucked it when I moved here." At the station, they called her a weather girl behind her back. It didn't matter that she held a PhD in Meteorology and could run rings around her colleagues. All they saw was her face and body.

"In September I'm starting at the National Weather Service here."

"Done," he said. Cinnamon didn't immediately follow Mac's comment until she felt him step away from her. It sunk in that he'd finished unbuttoning the dress. She wondered if his movement away from her had anything to do with the current that she felt.

Did he feel it, too?

She turned around quickly, facing him and careful to keep her naked back out of his view. He was taller than she thought and closer, too. She had to take a second step back to move out of his personal space and to break the...attraction between them. "I'll put it in the bag and bring it right down." Her voice was lower than normal, sexy, like a singer who's spent too many nights in smoky cafés.

Without acknowledgment, MacKenzie turned and went down the hall to the stairs. She stood still, listening to his footsteps on the soft carpeting until she could no longer hear them. Then she let out her breath, nearly bending over to let the air she was holding escape. Cinnamon was definitely losing it. She didn't even know this man and he'd come in angry, practically accusing her of stealing his sister's wedding gown. Why had she reacted to him like he was the last man on earth?

Being careful not to tear the dress, she quickly stepped out of it and slipped into the skirt and leggings she'd been wearing. She rehung the gown, replacing the tissue paper that had been stuffed in each sleeve. Zipping the bag closed, she took a deep breath and carried the dress down the steps to the bride's brother.

Her party dress, the purple strapless one, that MacKenzie Grier had brought with him was no longer lying haphazardly on the sofa, but had been hung from the molding above the pocket doors leading to the dining room. MacKenzie Grier was in the living room looking at the photos on the piano her grandmother used to play. Cinnamon had a vague memory of seeing her sitting there. Mac was holding a frame containing a picture of her and her sister, Samara. It had been taken the summer they were twelve.

She and Samara were only eleven months apart. They were actually half sisters, but neither ever referred to themselves as such. They shared a father and while Samara had been a source of irritation for Cinnamon's mother, her existence being proof of their father's philandering, the two girls got along famously.

"Let me apologize again," Cinnamon said, dropping thoughts of her parents and returning to the issue at hand. "It's a beautiful gown and I shouldn't have tried it on. I've never had a wedding gown on before and I wanted to…" She stopped speaking at the way he stared at her. His eyes were troubled and angry, but there was something else in them, something that was as confusing to Cinnamon as her reaction to him had been. She looked at the bag in her hands to keep from having to see those eyes. "I'm rambling," she said. "You have better things to do than listen to me. I hope your sister's wedding is as beautiful as the gown."

She handed him the dress and went toward the door, suddenly wanting him out of her house. His presence was huge and overwhelming. Cinnamon had never met a man like him, one whose air was that of command, whose confidence and control were visibly physical and one whose touch melted her skin. He should be wearing a policeman's uniform, or a drill sergeant's. She hadn't reacted to a man's hands like that...ever.

Mac slammed the back door of the car with a force that was the opposite of the careful attention he'd used to place Allison's dress on the back seat. Then yanking the driver's door open, he got in and started the engine. Music from the CD blared to life. He cut the engine, silencing it, and slumped back against the leather upholstery.

What was wrong with him? He'd practically taken Zahara Lewis's granddaughter's head off over a dress. It was wrong of her to try it on. That, she had admitted. But why did he flare up like a sunspot erupting?

It had to be the gown. The wedding dress. The whole idea of weddings irritated him. Mac hated weddings. He hated everything associated with promising 'til death do us part.

No one could really make a promise like that. People changed from day to day. How could they promise to stay together for a lifetime? He knew from firsthand experience that people could, and *would*, change their minds.

And did.

Jerrilyn McGowan had proved it to him, and she'd done it the hard way. They'd met at a fund-raiser and fallen immediately in love. At least Mac had thought it was love. Within months they were engaged and she seemed excited about all the wedding plans. He'd been excited, too. Jerrilyn had appeared fine, happy even. Then the night before the wedding, everything changed. The story he got was that at her bachelorette party several jokes were made about one man for life. With the wine and the song and the many men passing by the party's entrance, and poking their heads inside the hotel's party room, doubts formed in her mind. The next day, with the church full of guests and Mac waiting, she decided she wasn't ready for the one-man-for-life role.

She didn't show up for the wedding.

Instead she ran away. Mac hadn't seen her in two years. He knew she now lived in San Francisco where she moved after that fateful day. He was thankful for that. At least he didn't have to wonder if he was going to run into her at some Washington party. But the experience had soured him on both weddings and long-term relationships.

If it weren't for Allison, he'd never look at

another wedding gown or a bride. But she'd asked for his help and he'd do anything for her.

Without looking back at Zahara Lewis's house and its current resident, Mac put the car in gear and headed for his sister's. Yet he could still see Cinnamon's image in his mind. She was beautiful. The white lace made her brown skin glow. Her dark brown hair shone as it caressed her shoulders. He'd smelled the scent of her shampoo as his fingers fumbled with the beaded buttons of the dress. She had dark, intense eyes and luscious eyelashes. He'd tried not to look at her mouth, but his eyes were drawn there. She had perfect lips. As a newsman, Mac knew the sum total of a face and how far beauty could get someone. And Cinnamon's face confirmed the rule.

Mac shook himself, trying to dislodge his thoughts. He wanted nothing to do with Cinnamon Scott, just as he wanted nothing to do with a wedding.

Allison knew he wanted as little involvement in the wedding as possible. She knew he hated the entire idea. This was probably why she kept asking him to do things. He let her manipulate him, but there was a line and he was nearing it.

When this affair was over, he wanted nothing to do with another marriage, but the fates weren't listening to his wishes these days. He already had another invitation he couldn't refuse.

Only two years separated his age from that of his younger sister. Consequently, they shared a lot of the same friends. In a town the size of Indian Falls, it was impossible not to. And of course, those friends would all remember Mac's fiasco wedding—no, his non-wedding—to Jerrilyn McGowan.

The thought of that humiliating day two years ago still produced a metallic taste in his mouth. He'd stood in the anteroom waiting for the service to begin. It was like Jerrilyn to be late for everything, so their wedding day was no different in his mind. When an hour went by, he got nervous. She was never more than forty-five minutes late for anything. But it was their wedding and supposedly women needed more preparation that day than any other. Maybe her hair appointment ran late, or one of the bridesmaids didn't arrive on time. Any number of things could cause her to be late. The true reason—which Mac had refused to acknowledge—until the last possible moment was that she'd purposely jilted him.

He could hear the unrest in the sanctuary and while Richard Briscoe, Mac's best man and best friend, kept assuring him it was a woman thing, Mac somehow knew this was different.

Every few minutes Rick peered through the door and finally sighed with relief and turned to Mac.

"They're here," he said. "I just saw the brides-maids."

Mac sat down heavily on a chair. He'd been sweating. When Rick had said the bridesmaids were there, he'd breathed easier, but only for a moment. Jerrilyn's father joined them in the anteroom. He could see by the man's expression that something else was wrong.

Mac stood as he always did in the presence of Judge McGowan.

"Are we ready?" Mac asked.

His soon to be father-in-law didn't speak. The expression on his face said everything. Judge McGowan held out an envelope to Mac. He stared at it, but didn't take it. He *knew*. He'd known the moment he'd seen the judge's expression that Jerrilyn was not coming. Yet, Mac refused to believe this could be happening. She was here. Rick had said so.

"She's not coming, Mac," the judge said. "She said it would be a mistake to marry you when she's not in love with you."

He'd said it, made it real. Mac was stunned, numbed to the bone, but he looked into the judge's eyes. His future father-in-law looked ashamed, lost for words.

"I'll make the announcement," Rick said. "I think this is my job."

"I'll do it," the minister said. "I have had some experience in this area."

"No." Mac stopped them. "It has to be me." Mac knew he had to stand in front of a congregation of three hundred people and tell them he was being jilted. That the woman he had planned to share his life with would not be coming today or any day.

He took a step toward the door.

"Mac." The judge stopped him. Mac turned and found the judge had extended his hand. He knew Judge McGowan had not approved of his daughter's choice in a husband, but it seemed in the moment of their separation he'd found a new respect for Mac. Mac shook his hand. "I'm going with you," the judge said.

By mutual agreement the four men left the room....

Mac shivered suddenly in the warm summer air as he came back to the present. The car windows were down. The air was fresh and clear. He took a deep breath.

He never wanted to stand in front of a crowd again as the groom or part of a wedding party. But as he'd said, the fates were not with him. Not only was he part of his sister's wedding, he was her resident gopher for the hundreds of preparations that needed attention—like picking up her wedding gown and finding it on the wrong woman.

And Rick, his best man, was tying the knot later this summer. Mac was to stand up for him.

He found Allison in the kitchen drinking a glass of iced tea when he arrived at the house. On the table in front of her was a series of papers, plans for the wedding, details to check on. Her cell phone lay next to the papers indicating she was only taking a break from the tasks at hand.

"The dress," she said excitedly. "I'm so glad it's here. I've had nightmares that something would happen to it before the ceremony."

"That almost wasn't a nightmare," Mac said flatly.

"What do you mean?" Her eyes went to the white dress bag.

Mac hung the bag on the door that led to the center hall and unzipped it. Pulling it out, he held it up so Allison could see it. She rolled her wheelchair around and examined it. Mac then pushed it carefully back in the bag. He'd take it to her room in a moment.

"Don't worry, I made her take it off."

"Her?"

"Zahara Lewis's granddaughter."

"What? What does Zahara Lewis's grand-daughter have to do with my dress?"

Mac related the story of the mix-up. When he got to the shop to pick up his sister's gown, he'd found the delivery tickets had been switched and the delivery guy was already gone.

Mac went to the refrigerator and took out a bottle of beer. Twisting the top, he drank half the bottle in one long swallow. Leaning back against the counter, he looked at his sister. Usually her face was glowing with thoughts of her upcoming marriage. Now she looked confused.

Mac leaned against the refrigerator. "You should have seen her, Allison. Standing there, wearing your dress as if it was her own." Pushing himself up, he paced back and forth in front of her. She was calm. Too calm, he thought. Allison should be raging, angry over the audacity of a strange woman wearing the most important dress of her life. Yet she didn't seem to understand or grasp the meaning of his story.

Silence settled between them, but it was an uncomfortable silence. Allison looked intently at him.

"Why aren't you angry?" he asked. "I wanted to strangle Cinnamon Scott when I discovered her with your dress on."

"This isn't really about her, is it?" Allison said. "This is about Jerrilyn."

Mac stopped moving and his jaws clenched at the sound of his ex-fiancée's name. After two years he still couldn't control his reaction to the mention of her name. He stared at Allison, ready to say of course it was about Cinnamon Scott, but suddenly knew that wasn't true. Cinnamon Scott had looked gorgeous in that gown.

"She was the wrong woman for you, Mac. You know that," Allison continued. "In your heart, you know you and Jerrilyn would never have made it."

Mac said nothing. His sister could always see the truth. He hadn't loved Jerrilyn. She'd hurt his pride when she didn't show up for their wedding, but she'd really done him a favor. Yet knowing that didn't change his mind about weddings, women or relationships. He wanted no part of a serious relationship and the idea of a wedding made him sweat.

It didn't matter how beautiful Cinnamon Scott had looked. She was off-limits as far as he was concerned. He only wanted to deal with women who understood that no relationship would go further than the bedroom. There was no morning after, no breakfast, no discussion of another date, no future. It was here, now and nothing more.

Mac had loved Zahara Lewis. He should be prepared to respect her granddaughter, but his conversations with Zahara rarely included her granddaughters. When Mac saw Cinnamon, the adult, not the twelve-year-old in the photograph gracing the piano, but a full-grown bride, the kick to his stomach was nearly physical. Mac usually turned away from brides and talk of weddings, refusing to relive the events of that day two years earlier. But when he'd seen Cinnamon, none of that came to mind. He'd only seen how lovely she looked. She might be moving to Indian Falls, but he was surely going to spend more of his time in Washington.

Already he knew she was dangerous to his senses. He didn't want to think about the other places she could be dangerous. Or how he knew exactly which bedroom was hers.

Chapter 2

"Stop laughing." Cinnamon swiped the air with her fork. Samara moved back in mock terror. "That is not funny."

"You're right," Samara said. "It's hilarious. I can just see you, your hands scrambling trying to undo all those buttons."

Cinnamon could hardly keep a straight face at Samara's unbridled laughter. The humor of the situation was apparent, now that MacKenzie Grier wasn't standing in front of her, his glare as dark as midnight.

Cinnamon scanned the cafeteria. The place was crowded and busy at this hour. She heard several

American accents and as many foreign languages. Samara worked at the National Archives in downtown Washington, D.C. It was one of a dozen classical style buildings that composed the nation's capital. MacKenzie Grier had been the first thought on Cinnamon's mind when she woke up that morning. Pushing him aside, she did what she usually did when she was perplexed over something. She called her sister, Samara. Now she sat across from her in the cafeteria of one of the tourist infested eateries that seemed to be crowded year round, instead of only during Cherry Blossom season.

"You tried on another woman's wedding gown?" Samara's eyebrows raised in horror.

"Samara, you don't think you're the only person who's ever tried on one of the gowns in the store, do you?"

"Of course not, but the bride orders her gown. It's generally brand-new, never having been worn by another person. It's even bad luck—"

"Stop!" Cinnamon raised one hand. Her sister was superstitious and Cinnamon wasn't ready for another of her lectures. "Don't lecture me. I've had enough with MacKenzie Grier's piercing eyes pinning me to the wall."

"Ah, so he has piercing eyes." Samara changed tactics. A sly smile slid across her face as she popped a piece of lettuce from her salad in her mouth. "What color are they?"

"Brown, but the odds of you not knowing that are at least a billion to one."

"I know, I know," she conceded. "What about his voice? How did he sound to you?" She refused to give up.

"When he wasn't shouting at me, he had a normal voice. And why are you asking all these questions about him?" His voice wasn't normal. Not the normal kind that you wouldn't think of a second after you heard it. MacKenzie Grier had the kind of voice you listened to in the dark.

"Because you're my sister. You got a raw deal in Boston, but I know you really haven't given up on men."

"Oh, but you're wrong." Cinnamon rolled her eyes.

"Cinnamon, face it. You're in a male-dominated field. Even if you weren't, you can't avoid men. Pulling your hair in a bun and wearing no makeup won't prevent the opposite sex from finding you attractive. They'll see that gorgeous skin and long eyelashes and act like men."

"I'd never wear my hair in a bun."

"That's beside the point. Just look around." Samara spread her arms encompassing the room.

"I'll bet you couldn't get up to get a straw without every man in the room dogging your every step."

"So what was wrong with the men in Boston?"

"I'm still trying to figure that one out. I think they were afraid you'd show them up. And you never really met the right ones."

"Well, reporting the weather every day at six and eleven was not my idea of a long-term career. And with those hours it was hard to meet normal people. People outside of the newsroom or the weather bureau. Although there was Wesley Garner, but he's gone now." She stopped and took a drink of her wine. "I'm looking forward to the weather service."

"Don't forget about Mac."

"Mac?"

"Anyone named MacKenzie has got to be called Mac."

"How did he get back into this conversation?"

"Wasn't he the reason you came up here today?"

He was, Cinnamon thought, but Samara didn't know that. "I came to have lunch with you and to do some shopping."

"And…" Samara waved her hand indicating there was more that Cinnamon hadn't told her.

"And to tell you how angry I was at the way I was treated."

"Now that you're not angry anymore, what do you think of MacKenzie Grier? He's surely a hunk around this town."

"Oh my God!" Cinnamon nearly shouted.

"What?"

"I just realized who he is."

"You didn't know? All this time and you didn't realize he's the host of *Keeping it Honest?*" Samara started to laugh again.

Cinnamon thought a moment. His wasn't a show she watched regularly. The political scene wasn't her beat and when she wasn't at the station, she rarely watched television. Thinking about him, she remembered Mac's eyes. They were brown, a smooth milk chocolate color. They were expressive and mysterious. She remembered wondering about the multiple emotions she'd seen displayed there.

"Cinnamon, where are you?"

"I'm here." She had been distracted, but thought she'd keep her musings to herself.

"So, what's the answer to my question?" Samara asked.

Of course, Samara wasn't going to let her off the hook.

"I'm taking the fifth."

"Coward," she muttered.

"I'm not a coward, but I am observant." Cinnamon gazed around the room, but she continually came back to one man who averted his eyes each time she looked at him. Samara had said it was impossible for a male not to find her attractive. The male staring at them did not have his eyes on her. He was looking at her sister.

"What does that mean?"

"It means a certain young man hasn't taken his eyes off you since we sat down."

"Who?" she asked, turning around to look at the room. She saw him and turned her head. "Oh, him."

"Who is he?"

Samara made a face. "I've seen him around, but I haven't the slightest idea who he is."

"So, you're taking the fifth, too."

The Stafford Cafeteria was a good place to eat if you wanted simple, substantial food and were doing a paper on the eating habits and table manners of families of tourists visiting the nation's capital. It wasn't even on Mac's second or third list of places to go. He preferred the ambiance of upper Wisconsin Avenue or the serenity he felt by watching the slowly flowing waters through the windows of seafood restaurants along the Potomac River.

Justin Beckett had asked to meet him at the
Stafford. Why, was still a mystery, but Beckett
had slipped him a clue or two in the past and he
was a reliable source. The noise level was high and
activity seemed to be everywhere; people moving
back and forth, kids playing in food or trying to
get away from parents who were holding them in
line or in seats. Mac spotted Beckett sitting at a
table near the end of the room.

Approaching him, he said, "Beckett, I hope you
have a really good reason for bringing me to this
tourist trap." Mac hung a leg over a chair and sat
down in front of Justin Beckett.

"I do," he said.

Mac had been a reporter for several years. He
wrote a weekly editorial on the politics and politicians in Washington. Beckett worked in the
OEM, Office of Emergency Management. Like
the White House, the lights at OEM burned 24-7.
Most people didn't want to know what went on
there, even if they thought they did. Mac's actions
stopped. He'd never received an exclusive before
and wasn't sure if he was about to be delivered one
today.

"Well, what is it?" Mac asked. It wasn't often
that people came right out with what they wanted
to tell him. Some wanted graft. Some wanted to

drag out their secret, giving the appearance of self-importance, inflate their egos, until Mac either paid them or got up to walk away. Invariably that tactic would have them grasping his arm and trying to negotiate a deal. Beckett wasn't either type. He was usually straightforward. Honest. And Mac liked him a lot.

Beckett looked around to see if anyone was listening. "There's something going on up on the Hill."

There was always something going on up on the Hill. Mac forced himself not to say it. "Something more than the usual?"

Justin Beckett nodded. He leaned forward and whispered. "I don't know how many people are involved."

Mac felt his blood pressure rising. It always happened when he smelled something big. Excitement flowed through him.

"I only overheard a little bit of it, but the pages are part of it."

"What is it?" Mac couldn't help asking. Beckett was drawing this out too long. They were sitting in a very public place. Anyone could see them. Maybe that was why Beckett had chosen it. It was touristy and not apt to be serving a single government official, outside the paid security guards.

"I wish I knew. I was on the Hill this morning. I go there every now and then."

"Just like you have lunch here?"

"There's another reason for that." Beckett glanced over Mac's shoulder. Mac didn't follow his gaze. If someone was there who shouldn't see them, he wouldn't draw their attention. He would find out who it was later.

"What happened on the Hill?"

"Like I said, I go there occasionally. For no real reason except to relax, stand in the place where history was made. I join the public tour."

Mac smiled. Beckett was a lot like him.

"You never know what you'll hear or see. What I heard this morning was totally unexpected. I was standing at the John Adams desk in the Rotunda."

Mac nodded. He knew about the desk. John Adams is the only President of the United States who ever returned to Congress after being president. And for a very good reason. Through some trick of construction in the former Senate chamber, if something was whispered at a particular spot on the other side of the room, the words could be heard as clear as if they were spoken directly to him at his desk. Adams never revealed this secret, but he used the knowledge he'd heard politically to get what he wanted.

"I overheard one of the Congressional pages talking about a cover-up."

"Which page? What cover-up? And what was a page doing in the Rotunda?"

"I don't know. He didn't give any names or details."

"Then he could have been talking about the plot of a book or a television program he saw the night before."

Beckett was already shaking his head. "It was the tone in which he said it that made me believe he was talking about something involving one of the senators."

"Justin, there's nothing here. What do you expect me to do with this?"

"I don't know." He spread his hands. "You're the only reporter I trust. Maybe you can just keep your eyes and ears open and see what develops."

Mac wasn't an investigative reporter. He did political commentary. But he still needed sources to find out the hidden motivation behind decisions made on the Hill. Motivation was often the subject of discussion on his show.

"Mac?" Beckett said.

"I'll check around and see what I can find out," Mac said after a moment. He was disappointed. He was expecting something big and he got nothing. Cover-ups in this town were as plentiful as tourists.

Beckett was looking over Mac's shoulder again. Turning in his chair, Mac followed Beckett's gaze. His breath caught when he saw Cinnamon Scott sitting in a booth about three tables in front of them. There was a big smile on her face as she laughed at something another woman said to her. What was she doing here?

"You know Cinnamon Scott?" Mac asked.

"Who's Cinnamon Scott?"

Mac turned around again. This time he looked at the other woman. The two had the same color hair, but nothing else about them spoke of a blood-relationship. Yet Mac knew the woman was Samara. There were photos of her at Zahara's. Cinnamon had spoken of her yesterday. Mac remembered holding the photo of the two of them. Both had filled out nicely compared to the twelve-year-olds they were in the photograph. His eyes went back to Cinnamon. At that moment hers connected with his and the smile on her face froze.

"Samara?" he asked Beckett.

"You know her?" His eyebrows rose. "I should have known you'd know every beautiful woman in D.C."

Mac accepted the compliment which he thought

of as an insult. He did not know every woman and was by no means a playboy. Granted he never wanted for companionship, but he didn't love 'em and leave 'em, either.

"Many people believe Washington is a big place, but in actuality, it's very small," he told Beckett.

"How did you meet her?" Beckett asked. "She works here and she's not in the news. I believe she even shies away from the spotlight."

"Samara's grandmother and I come from the same town." Samara had visited Zahara a couple of times since Mac had lived in her house. Yet the two hadn't crossed paths. By coincidence, he'd been away during her visits. "But, it's her sister I've met," Mac said drily. "She's the other woman sitting with her." Mac's cell phone rang and he turned back, pulling it out of his jacket pocket. "Excuse me," he said to Beckett before answering the call. After a moment he closed the tiny instrument and returned it to his pocket. "Sorry, but I have to go."

"Trouble?" Beckett asked.

"Nothing serious, but I have to run." Mac got up. Beckett stood, too, lifting the plastic tray his lunch had been on. "I'll keep a watch out for anything on the Hill," Mac promised.

Mac glanced at Cinnamon and her sister. She

winced as he and Beckett got up and walked
toward them. It gave him a perverted sense of
pleasure that he made her uncomfortable. He also
felt an unfamiliar clench in his stomach and an
overall feeling of happiness at seeing her. The urge
to go over and slip into the booth next to her was
strong, but he had somewhere to be. And the image
of Cinnamon in the wedding gown was still in his
mind, fighting with the image of her bare back as
he unhooked the dress buttons.

Mac's office was crowded with papers. His
computer was practically lost among the many
newspapers and magazines he read each day. He
needed to read everything on the political scene in
order to select his guests and prepare discussion
questions. He sat at his desk. He'd followed up on
Beckett's comments. The last person he'd called
had just hung up. Mac replaced the phone and
turned around and stared out the window. The view
only showed him the buildings across the street
from his office. He thought about the calls he'd
made, but nothing seemed of any use. He'd keep
an ear open to what Beckett said. Something might
develop. Mac had feelers out, people he could
trust.

What was she doing there? His mind went to

Cinnamon Scott. She was the last person Mac expected to see, especially in a tourist cafeteria. But since he'd laid eyes on her, he couldn't get her out of his mind. She had a great smile. He grinned, just thinking about it. She hadn't bestowed her smile on him, but in the cafeteria with her sister, the two had laughed at something. Mac hoped it wasn't him.

"What are you doing? Aren't you supposed to be working?"

Mac turned around and saw Ebon Massey standing before his desk. Ebon had been Mac's mentor. He knew everything there was to know about the news, especially Washington news, but his sphere of influence extended well beyond the District's boundaries. And he always greeted Mac with a joke.

"Hi, Ebon, I was just thinking."

"About whom?" Ebon took a seat. "That didn't look like a 'finding the perfect guest for the show' look."

It wasn't, Mac thought to himself. Then he decided to ask Ebon. "Have you ever heard of someone named Cinnamon Scott from Boston?"

"Did the weather for the last few years," Ebon stated as if he were a walking computer. "She's beautiful and doesn't do much in the political arena. Where'd you meet her?"

"Her house," Mac said.

"Are you interested in her?"

"No," Mac said, probably too quickly.

"Then why are you asking about her?"

"I ran into her last weekend. She's moved to Indian Falls, and she'll start working for the NWS at the end of summer."

Ebon raised his brows. "That ought to be interesting."

"What?" Mac asked.

"You, interested in a woman who might want more from you than one night of passion."

"I'm not interested in her," he protested. "She now owns the house where I used to live. I'm staying with my sister and I wondered if she'd be open to selling it to me." Mac latched onto a reason to justify his interest in Cinnamon, if that's what it was.

Ebon gave him a pointed look. "Why don't you make her an offer?"

"I have. She turned it down."

"So what else will you do?"

"I thought if I found out why she left Boston, she might want to return there and then I could buy the house."

"Why that house? There must be other properties you could buy in that area."

Ebon was in his late sixties. His hair was white and he packed a few more pounds than his doctor thought was healthy, but his mind was as perceptive as it had been in his prime.

"I like having roots there. I stayed with the previous owner for a while. She treated me like a son. I feel I owe her."

"But Ms. Scott is a blood relative. Don't you think she already has roots in the house and she'll take care of it?"

"Indian Falls is a small town. Cinnamon Scott is from Boston. And she hasn't been to visit her grandmother since she was about twelve years old. Her roots are not in that house."

Ebon got up. "You have roots here, too," Ebon reminded him. "Your parents left you a house."

"Us," he said. "They left *us* a house, my sister and me. Since she's getting married, and the house is outfitted with all the handicap devices Allison needs, it's better if she keeps the house."

"I still say there are other houses in that area. There's something else on your mind. I'm not even sure you understand it." He paused, then said, "Yet."

"What does that mean?"

"I don't know. But you'll figure it out." Then he took a step toward the door. "I came in to ask you for the Wendell report. Could you e-mail it to me?"

"Sure," Mac said. "Right away."

He turned to his computer as Ebon left and sent the report to him. Then he stared at the screen. His reflection on it was mirrored back at him. Was he trying to get rid of Cinnamon? He knew the answer to that. He didn't want her there, didn't want her staying in Zahara's house. She hadn't been there for her grandmother when she was alive. Coming in now and taking over the house seemed like a slap in Zahara's face.

Mac remembered her opening her home to any and everyone who came by. Often a crowd would drop by just to say hello, enjoy a television program or sit on the wide porch and talk. Mac felt comfortable there. He worked without her interference. She never asked him about his plans to come and go, yet there was a ready-made meal for him when he got in.

The only surprise Mac had was why Zahara had left the house to Cinnamon alone and not to both her granddaughters. If she was going to leave it to one of them, Mac thought, it should have been Samara. She was the one who had come to visit her. But as he'd seen in life, it rarely goes the way you expect.

After all, he never expected to find Cinnamon wearing a wedding gown.

* * *

The wind blew through the car windows and ruffled Cinnamon's hair. She pushed it back without thought. Her eyes were trained on the road, but she'd traveled it often enough in the last several months that she could do it mindlessly.

And that's what she was doing. Her thoughts were on MacKenzie Grier. He hadn't even had the decency to acknowledge her with a nod. But then, why should she think he would? He'd been so rude the first time she'd met him. Why should she expect his actions to be any different the next time she saw him?

Grabbing her blowing hair, she pushed it behind her ear and leaned her arm on the window ledge. Determined to force him out of her mind, she concentrated on the scenery. The trees along the highway were beautiful as spring blended into summer. Cinnamon loved this drive. She liked Indian Falls with its separated houses and streets where people strolled and enjoyed the scenery instead of rushing past it to get from point A to point B.

Slowing down as she reached the limits of the town, Cinnamon hadn't quite achieved her goal of forgetting MacKenzie Grier. Pulling into her driveway, she was surprised to find a dark-green van sitting there. She didn't recognize it and she wasn't expecting anyone. She also wasn't in the mood for visitors. Glancing at the van, she saw no one in the driver's seat, but when she went around the car and headed for the porch she stopped short.

"Hello," she said, walking up the four steps to the wraparound porch. Sitting near the door was a woman in a wheelchair. "How did you get up here?" Cinnamon frowned. The house had no handicap ramp.

"I can walk a little," the woman said, "and my fiancé brought the chair up."

Cinnamon glanced around, looking toward the van and wondered why he wasn't waiting with her.

"He's taking a walk," she answered as if she understood the unasked question. "I'm Allison Grier." She offered her hand to Cinnamon.

Cinnamon reached to take it, when the name registered. "Allison Grier," she repeated. MacKenzie Grier's sister.

The bride.

For the second time in two days, Cinnamon's stomach dropped. Thankfully, all she was carrying was her purse and it was slung over her shoulder.

"I am so sorry," Cinnamon apologized. "The dress was so beautiful, like lacy ice cream and marshmallows. I didn't mean to do anything to it—"

"I'm not here about the dress." Allison held her hand up for Cinnamon to stop.

"You're not?"

She shook her head. There was a big smile on her face. Cinnamon estimated her age to be close to her own twenty-nine years. She wore a yellow sun dress and had smooth skin. Yellow was a good color on her. It highlighted the light brown of her skin. Her eyes were dark-brown and could be as piercing as her brother's, but they were soft and happy right now. She sat up straight in the chair, yet a wave of pity went through Cinnamon at her inability to run and dance.

"I thought it was high time I came by and met Zahara Lewis's granddaughter. With all the details of the wedding going on, I've had little time for anything else."

"Do you have time to come in for a cup of coffee?"

"I'd like that."

Twenty minutes later they were seated in Cinnamon's kitchen each with a cup in front of her. Cinnamon had moved a chair from the table to allow room for Allison's wheelchair.

"Do you think it's bad luck, too? I mean that I tried your gown on?"

"Let me put your mind to rest. I believe in my

fiancé. His name is Paul. Paul Mathis. No dress will determine our future."

"Your brother was adamant. I've never seen anyone so angry." Cinnamon smiled as she remembered the look on his face and the darkness that painted his skin when he saw her.

"He can be quite protective."

Cinnamon looked at the wheelchair and knew he must have spent a lot of time helping her.

"I'm sure he was very rude, too," Allison stated.

Cinnamon covered her reaction by sipping from her cup. "Only a little," she lied.

Allison gave an uproarious laugh. "My brother never does anything *little*." She took a moment to look around the kitchen. "I see you haven't changed much."

"I haven't been here that long. And it appears my grandmother updated some of the rooms in the last few years."

"She did. Mac can tell you a lot about that. He was here for most of it. Mac even did some of the work. He can be handy when he wants to. Did all the work at our house for years. Luckily, Paul is also handy."

"Here?" That was all Cinnamon heard. Something rushed inside her like a tickle in her blood. She couldn't explain it, and quickly pushed it away.

"He'd come to town a few times a month and he always stayed here. Paul and I were living together and he said he felt like a third wheel, so Zahara offered him a room anytime he wanted one. He's written many of his columns right here."

"Which room?" Cinnamon asked. Her mind flashed back to the day when he'd come to her bedroom door. At first she thought he'd followed the sound of her voice, but now she wondered if he didn't know exactly where he was going.

"I don't know."

"Did he have a key?"

She nodded. "He wanted to buy the place, but discovered Zahara had left it to you. He turned the key in to the lawyer right after he cleared all his stuff out."

Cinnamon had been given many keys, some loose, some on rings or chains. It came as a surprise that one of them was MacKenzie Grier's. And he'd wanted to buy the house.

"So, how do you like my brother?" Allison interrupted her thoughts.

"We haven't really met," Cinnamon hedged the question. "For the most part he only glared and shouted at me. And my seeing him in D.C. didn't forge a good opinion, either."

"You saw him today?" Her eyebrows went up.

"I met my sister for lunch and by coincidence he happened to be meeting with someone in the same cafeteria."

"Justin Beckett."

Cinnamon nodded. "We weren't introduced."

"What did he do?"

"Nothing. He didn't so much as acknowledge my presence, although he looked me straight in the eye."

"I'm sure he had something on his mind."

Cinnamon remembered he'd just taken a phone call, but that was no reason to look through a person. Since she'd come here to Indian Falls where people went out of their way to be friendly, she'd quickly become used to nods, waves and smiles. Back in D.C. she could only suppose Mac had fallen back into his cosmopolitan persona, yet that didn't account for him not speaking to someone he knew.

"Let me make it up to you," Allison said. "I'd like you to come to my wedding."

"What? Why?"

"Well, you're new in town, Zahara was a special friend, you like my dress and I have the feeling we're going to be very good friends."

Cinnamon smiled at her. She liked Allison Grier almost as much as she disliked her brother. Allison produced a white envelope and pushed it across the table toward her.

"You're welcome to bring a guest."

Cinnamon smiled as she took it. "I promise to wear something other than white lace."

to cry anymore. Even married to my seven
I doubt our marriage of the couple to make
the wedding day, until that ministers

Chapter 3

Cinnamon loved weddings. She wasn't one to cry. For her, weddings were happy days. She loved the bridesmaids floating down the aisle past flower-decorated pews. She loved the colors, the happiness and the combining of lives. The ambiance of the day seemed to put all the world's problems on hold as the happy couple made their vows before friends and loved ones. Cinnamon believed in finding Mr. Right and living happily ever after. Despite her parents' breakup and her mother—now between husbands, but Cinnamon was sure number four lurked somewhere waiting to be found—Cinnamon still believed in marriage.

Allison Grier's wedding had been perfect, and the weather cooperated for the outdoor reception. The sky was blue with huge billowing clouds, soft as cotton and mindful of a bride's bouquet. Everyone smiled and kissed. Only Mac looked like he was attending a funeral and not a wedding. His face was slightly more relaxed now that the ceremony was over, but in the church he'd been visibly nervous. Cinnamon wondered why he appeared so uncomfortable. It wasn't his wedding, and everything had gone off without a hitch.

In the last few years, Cinnamon had attended several weddings. This was the order of things, her mother used to tell her. After college comes wedding showers, then baby showers, then divorce. Then more marriages. Cinnamon had added the last thinking of her mother's three trips to the altar. Her father had only been married twice. Cinnamon was the product of his first marriage and her sister Samara came from the second.

Samara was Cinnamon's guest. The two sisters didn't get to spend much time together when Cinnamon was in Boston, and after Samara called to say she wanted to come for the weekend, it was natural to invite her to attend the wedding, too. Besides, Cinnamon had the distinct feeling that although Allison said she could invite a guest, she really didn't want her to bring someone of the opposite sex. Her comment about her brother set Cinnamon's teeth on edge. Was Allison trying to play Cupid? If she was, she should have chosen someone who hadn't been on the receiving end of Mac Grier's anger.

Twice.

What could Mac have told her to give her the impression that the two of them even wanted to be in each other's company? Cinnamon gave up trying to figure out the machinations of the Grier family's minds. It was too nice a day to be bothered with something that didn't really concern her.

Cinnamon looked over the yard. The Grier house was totally different from the one Cinnamon now lived in. Her grandparents had had it built fifty years ago, giving it a distinct Australian Outback look. They'd lived in Australia for several years while her grandfather served as ambassador to that country. The Grier house was mansion-style, with white columns and a porticoed entrance. The reception was in the backyard which was normally a huge flower garden. Today, white table-clothed tables with colorful centerpieces that matched the peach and pink bridesmaids gowns and coordinating place settings, decorated the space.

"Do you know any of these people?" Samara asked. She was scanning the area. "There must be at least two hundred guests. We should know someone."

"*You* should know someone," Cinnamon said. "You came here often. Except for moving back when grandmother left me the house, I haven't been here since before the divorce."

"Well, I know Fletcher Caton. He owns a gift shop on Main Street." Samara smiled as Fletcher nodded to her. "And Mrs. Sweeney over there."

"I know Amanda, too," Cinnamon said. Amanda owned the bridal shop that had delivered the wrong gown and brought the wrath of Mac Grier down on Cinnamon's head.

"I mean, do we know any eligible males that are here?"

Cinnamon surveyed the tables. She smiled. "We should. There are a lot of them here, including him."

Samara looked in the direction Cinnamon indicated. "What is *he* doing here?" she asked, with a frown.

"I imagine he's a friend of the family. He was at lunch that day I visited you."

"Yeah, he always seems underfoot."

"*Really?*" Cinnamon's eyebrows rose as she stared at her sister.

"Don't go there, Cinnamon. He's the last man on earth I want to have anything to do with."

The wedding party arrived amid fanfare from the guests. Cinnamon looked up as they took their places at the head table. She smiled at the grace of their movements, at how Allison's husband tended to her, how the bridesmaids and grooms-men assumed the arrangement of seats. Then her eyes alighted on MacKenzie Grier. At the same moment, he spotted her.

By the look on his face, Allison had failed to mention the invitation to him.

"I'll be right back," Samara said. She got up and went over to speak to some of the guests that she'd met previously. Despite saying she knew no one, there were people she recognized. Samara's mother didn't have the same experience with their father's family that Cinnamon's mother had had. Or if she had, she'd put it behind her.

Cinnamon sat alone at the table that had been assigned to her. Mac's stare was direct and pene-trating. It made Cinnamon sweat, but she refused to back away from him. Instead she stood up, spread her arms and turned in a complete circle, showing him the light-yellow dress that she wore. It had no lace, no sleeves and no train.

He turned away from her and Cinnamon laughed out loud.

"What's so funny?" Samara asked, returning to the table.

"Mac just saw me."

"Good." She smiled brightly looking toward the head table.

"Apparently not. I don't think he knew we were on the guest list."

"He was just surprised."

"Samara, don't make excuses. There is nothing between the two of us. Our first meeting wasn't anything to write home about and the day I had lunch with you, he didn't so much as look in my direction."

Samara took a drink from her water glass. "A sure sign that he's interested."

Cinnamon rolled her eyes. "Samara, you can't just make it happen."

"What?"

"Don't give me that innocent look." Cinnamon mocked her. "I'm off men and you know it."

"You can't make a blanket statement like that."

"Why not? It's my life. I can live it the way I want. It's a right I'm guaranteed by the Constitution."

"Boston isn't the world, Cinnamon."

"No, but it's a large part of it."

"Cinnamon, you have to let it go," Samara said, slightly perturbed with her. "You can't swear off men because of one bad relationship."

"It wasn't one."

"No, but they were all wrong for you." Samara turned and stared at her. "You're going to hate me for this, but you're acting like your mother."

"I am not!"

"She's always searching for the right man and so are you. The difference is she takes the chance and marries them. You find a reason to push them away."

Cinnamon felt slapped. "Do I really do that?"

"Not consciously," Samara said, her tone comforting. "What you need to do is let yourself go a little. Don't look for a reason to end a relationship. Stick it out and see where it leads you. It may go nowhere, but it might be the one you're looking for."

"You're always so sure of yourself. But for me, finding Jarrod with another woman was the last straw."

"Don't let his idiocy ruin your chances, Cinnamon. If you do, he wins."

"Wins?"

"Of course, he moves on and you're left standing in his dust. You know men love that. They want you home pining away for them. The best thing you can do is replace him immediately. And who better to do it with than him?" Samara sighed. "Look at him, Cinnamon." She glanced toward Mac. "He's gorgeous. Even better looking than when he's on TV."

As much as Cinnamon didn't want to look, she couldn't help it. Mac *was* good-looking. In his tuxedo, he was as dashing as a swashbuckler. And just as dangerous, she reminded herself. He smiled at something someone said to him. His face totally changed at that moment. His eyes crinkled and his features relaxed. Cinnamon smiled as if she were part of the conversation. His eyes locked with hers and she quickly turned away.

"Good-looking men are plentiful," she said to Samara. "I worked with a score of them."

"But none of them set you off like he does." Again she nodded toward the front of the yard.

"Set me off? What are you talking about?"

"I'm talking about the way you look at him when you don't think anyone is watching. The way your eyes seek him out as if he was as delicious as chocolate candy."

"I don't do that."

Cinnamon turned to her sister whose head was already nodding.

"I've seen him all of three times, including today. Even I need more time than that to go goo-goo eyes over a man."

Cinnamon looked at Mac again. At least where he'd been sitting. His chair was empty. She looked around the yard trying to spot him. When she'd canvassed the entire space and her eyes met her sister's, the smirk on her face couldn't have said "I told you so" better than if she'd spoken the words aloud.

The waiters began serving the meal. Samara and Cinnamon talked to their neighbors until the other marriage rituals began, the best man's toast and the bride and groom's first dance as man and wife. Paul lifted Allison from her chair and the couple danced several steps. The crowd applauded. Cinnamon tried not to look for Mac, but when he appeared near the front table, she saw him retake his seat. She told herself she wasn't really looking *for* him. She didn't want to be surprised by him showing up suddenly and accusing her of some other infraction of his rules.

Couples joined the bride and groom on the floor that had been laid out over the grass in front of a small band. Samara was immediately asked to dance. Cinnamon envied her sister. She was a butterfly in a room full of owls. Someone always wanted her hand. Like the man in the cafeteria who couldn't keep his eyes off her.

Mac danced with one of the bridesmaids. Cinnamon looked away and found Fletcher Caton coming toward her.

"How about a dance?" he asked.

Cinnamon got up. The card-and-gift–store owner was old enough to be her father, yet Cinnamon found him extremely light on his feet. She enjoyed dancing with him and smiled as he twirled her around the floor in what had to be a dance they did during one of the wars. She wasn't sure which one, but it wasn't one she'd lived through. Catching Samara's eye, she smiled widely as they shared a private joke.

From Fletcher she danced with several of the groomsmen and finally the groom. Mac hadn't even looked in her direction. Why it irritated her, she couldn't say. Maybe some of what Samara had said was true. Cinnamon dreamed of her own wedding, but each time she got anywhere near it, it seemed her relationships deteriorated. Was she really unconsciously putting up roadblocks due to her mother's marriage history?

Paul turned her around to the music. Cinnamon thought of Jarrod. She'd thought he was the one. Mr. Right. She'd envisioned them dancing at their own wedding. Plans of shopping for wedding gowns, invitations, choosing a ring had all gone through her head. And then she'd discovered the truth. Jarrod wasn't in love with her. She found him in a wild embrace with someone she didn't know. And then he told her he didn't love her.

That had been when she'd sworn off men. Jarrod had been the final straw. She didn't want anything more to do with them. The gibes at the office got to her after that and she jumped at the NWS job offer and moving to Indian Falls. It was a new start. Something she needed. She didn't know her move would bring her into the line of sight of Mac Grier. But she was here now and she wasn't backing down.

"Allison and I are very glad you could attend," Paul said, pulling her back to the present.

Cinnamon wondered how many times today he'd delivered that line. Instead of the obligatory thank-you, she said, "I was thrilled that Allison came to see me. I'm sure she told you about the dress."

"We had a good laugh over it. She also told me how Mac reacted. I apologize for that."

"Think nothing of it. I'm sure we've put it behind us."

He swung her around, his steps smooth and sure. Cinnamon couldn't help thinking how well he danced and how Allison would never be able to fully appreciate his expertise.

"Has Mac mentioned me?" She hoped her question was as innocent as she intended it to be.

"Not in my presence. Allison kept both of us very busy this last week. We were forever on the phone or running somewhere to check on details."

"Well, it worked," Cinnamon told him. "The day couldn't be better and the service was beautiful."

"And I'm having a wonderful time," Paul said. The music ended.

Cinnamon stepped out of his arms. They began walking off the floor. "Thank you," she said. "I can find my way back. And I know you have other guests to dance with." She turned to leave and found herself standing in front of Mac.

"Mr. Grier," she said.

"Mac," he corrected her.

"Mac," Cinnamon said. She moved to go around him, but he took her hand.

"Dance?" he asked, putting his arm around her waist as the music started up. He gave her no opportunity to refuse him as she would have. The hand on her waist was hot and heavy. She felt it burning through the fabric of her summer dress. Unlike dancing with Fletcher or Paul, she was stiff and awkward in his arms. "Relax," he said. "I won't bite you."

"Can I have that in writing?" Cinnamon asked.

"I am surprised to find you here. When I mailed the invitations, you weren't on the guest list."

"Would you like me to leave?" Cinnamon stopped dancing.

Mac pushed back and stepped on her toes. "Of course not," he said. She began to move again. "So are you going to tell me?"

"Tell you what?"

"Why you're crashing my sister's wedding."

She looked up at him with enough venom in her eyes to kill a small city. "Well, I wore the dress. It seemed only decent to attend the wedding." The music hadn't ended, but Cinnamon stepped out of his arms. "Mr. Grier, I think we should just shake hands and go our separate ways. It's obvious we have nothing to say to each other."

She left him, walking slowly so as not to create a scene. She'd never been so angry. How could he think she was low enough to crash a wedding? She looked around, searching. Where was Samara? She was leaving.

Now!

"Cinnamon."

She heard Mac call her name. Unmindful of him or anyone else who might be looking, she continued to walk around the perimeter of the yard. He caught her arm as she passed the house and guided her through a doorway and into an office.

"Let me go." Cinnamon jerked free of his hold. It wasn't very strong and she easily disengaged herself. Opening her purse, she extracted the envelope with her name clearly written in an elaborate script and thrust it into his hand. "Will this do?"

"Cinnamon Scott and Guest," he read.

She moved to go around him, but he stepped in front of her. "I didn't know."

"Is that an apology?"

"You could have told me you had an invitation while we were dancing."

"I guess that's a no?" What was it with men? Why couldn't they just acknowledge that they did something wrong and then go on. Cinnamon had apologized for trying on his sister's dress, yet he couldn't even admit he was wrong about her being at the wedding.

Mac sighed and took a step away from her. She relaxed a bit, too. She'd been holding her breath, only letting out small amounts of air.

"Look, it was an honest mistake," he said.

"Only on your part."

"All right, I admit it. I shouldn't have jumped to conclusions. I should have asked."

That's as close to an apology as she was going

to get. "Okay, Mr. Grier, I can give a little, too. We got started on the wrong foot. Why don't we just kiss, makeup and go our own way?"

"I like the kiss part," he said, so automatically that it insulted Cinnamon.

"Consider it done."

"Oh, no," he said, flashing her a smile. "I like my kisses actual, not virtual."

For a charged moment they stared at each other. Cinnamon had the feeling he really wanted to kiss her. But why? They'd been as compatible as fire and ice. So why did excitement cut through her at the mental picture of her mouth pressed to his and his arms locked around her?

She moved farther away from him, spotting a photograph on the bookcase behind the desk.

"Is this where you work when you're here?" She reached for something to distract her from the image. They stood in his office.

"Yes, why?"

She lifted the heavy frame and stared at the people facing the camera. In the center, between Mac and Allison stood her grandmother, Zahara Lewis. The photo had been taken in the living room of Cinnamon's house. Decorations hung from the walls in the background.

"It was her birthday, five years ago," Mac supplied. "We gave her a surprise party."

"I wish I'd known," she said absently, speaking to the grandmother she barely knew.

"We didn't know where to reach you."

Cinnamon turned around. Mac was a lot closer to her than she expected him to be. She backed up until she felt the bookcase behind her.

Turning, she replaced the photo. "Allison says you wanted to buy the house."

His face changed, as if he were an animal who'd hunted and finally had his prey in sight. "I still do. I can make you an offer right now."

"It's not for sale."

"I thought you might have changed your mind."

"Why would I do that? I have a job nearby and…"

"And what?" he prompted.

"And I want to know more about my grand-mother."

"Why didn't you come and visit her? You could have learned firsthand."

"It wasn't possible," Cinnamon answered.

"Why not?" He was menacingly close to her.

"It just wasn't, but I hear you spent a lot of time with her, even lived in her house."

"*Your* house," he corrected.

She nodded. Her throat was too dry for her to

speak. It was her house now. Knowing Mac had lived in the house made her nervous. Since Allison had mentioned it, Cinnamon thought of him each time she walked into a room. When she turned a light on, she wondered if his hand had done it before her.

In fact, for someone she disliked, he occupied a large portion of her thoughts.

"I think I'd better go find my sister," Cinnamon said. "And I'm sure you have best man duties to perform."

"Are we all made up now? Friends and neighbors?"

"Neighbors," she said.

As she moved to pass him, he took her arm and turned her to face him. "Kiss and make up," he said, and his mouth took hers. He kissed her hard, and Cinnamon clutched his arms. For a long moment, she hung there. Then, she regained her senses and jerked back, but he was still holding her.

"Let me go, Mr. Grier." She hoped he couldn't hear the pleading in her voice. Or feel the rapid beating of her heart.

"I'm not holding you," he said.

She looked down. His hands hung at his sides, but hers were on his waist. When had she put them there? She dropped them quickly, but didn't want to. She wanted to keep them there, run them up his body. Her palms itched with the warmth of him. She could still feel the pressure of his hands holding her close, the imprint of his body against hers and the dark secret of his mouth.

Mac's hand came up and slowly lifted her chin until she was staring into his eyes.

"I think you know me well enough to call me Mac now."

Chapter 4

"Wake up, sleepyhead."

Cinnamon groaned as she opened her eyes. Samara came through the bedroom door. Cinnamon closed her eyes and turned her face into the pillow. "Go away," she moaned.

"How's your head?"

"I left it somewhere. And I don't know where that is."

"Well, open your eyes. I brought help."

Cinnamon peered up.

"Coffee," Samara said. "Elixir of the gods." She sat Indian-style on the coverlet and put a breakfast tray in front of her.

Cinnamon pushed herself up against the pillows. Raising her hand to her head, she tried to contain the pounding. She took the coffee cup her sister offered and tested the liquid for heat before drinking it.

"How much did you drink last night?" Samara asked.

"I didn't count."

"You rarely drink more than a couple of glasses of wine. So was it Mac Grier who's putting you on the road to Margaritaville?"

Cinnamon stared over her coffee cup. "I am not on the road to Margaritaville."

"Don't give me that look," Samara told her, lowering her chin and mocking her sister. "I've seen it before and it has no effect on me."

Cinnamon cut her eyes away, looking into her cup again.

"Here, have some toast." Samara offered her a plate.

Cinnamon couldn't think of eating anything.

"It'll make you feel better."

She took the buttered bread and bit off a small piece. Samara was eating like she hadn't had breakfast in years.

"What happened to you last night? You were dancing with that guy."

"What guy?" Samara asked. Cinnamon wasn't

so out of it that she didn't realize her sister was feigning ignorance.

"The one from the cafeteria. The one you don't like. The one who's always underfoot."

"Well, he *can* dance." She smiled. "But I didn't spend any time with him. I was too busy making sure you didn't make a fool of yourself."

"I didn't have to. Allison Grier, excuse me, Allison Mathis, made sure of that."

Cinnamon looked at the chair in the corner. Lying across it was the dress she'd worn to the ceremony and reception. On a small table next to it was the bridal bouquet.

When they called for all the single women to gather for the traditional throwing of the bride's bouquet, Cinnamon had remained at a nearby table where she was talking to the groom's mother. She was off men. She didn't need to participate in any superstitious act just because she was single. She had no plans to change her marital status.

Allison rolled her wheelchair to the center of the dance floor. The crowd of women stood behind her. The gathering had become quiet, waiting for her to throw the bouquet. Cinnamon saw Allison glance at her brother and wink. Then, calling Cinnamon's name, she flung the bouquet at her. To protect herself, Cinnamon caught the flowers.

All eyes were on her as the sound of happiness and sorrow rose from the crowd of women. Cinnamon stole a glance at Mac. His face had turned as bright a red as it could under the darkness of his skin.

"I guess this means you're next." Samara's voice brought her back to the present.

"Next for what?"

"For marriage, of course."

"Samara, you're the superstitious one. And how many times has that worked? Most people who catch the bouquet are not the next ones to marry."

"We'll see," she said in an irritating manner. Unfolding her legs, she got off the bed. "Eat up. I have to go back now."

"Already? What time is it?" Cinnamon looked at the clock radio. Her eyes opened wide. It was nearly noon.

"I want to get back to the city before the traffic gets bad." Washington, D.C., traffic was known for being notoriously gridlocked. "I've put everything in the car. I'll call you when I get home."

Samara hugged her and with a bright smile, she was gone. The house felt empty the moment Cinnamon heard her sister's car engine recede. Pushing the covers back, she pulled the tray closer and finished the breakfast Samara had cooked. Her head felt a lot better after eating.

Getting out of bed, she switched on the television, needing the noise. As the screen jelled into faces, Mac Grier stared at her.

Good morning, I'm MacKenzie Grier and this is Keeping it Honest.

Cinnamon dove for the television remote and hit the off switch. She wasn't ready to see him right now. And she wasn't ready for honesty. She still had Mac's kiss on her mouth, even though she'd tried to wash it away with Margaritas.

According to the sign at the city limit, Indian Falls had a population of 3,259. Cinnamon walked down Main Street, stopping briefly to look in the shop windows. She would never do this in Boston. There, it was a rush, rush place. You only went out if you needed something. If you shopped, it was at a mall.

Allison's wedding was behind her. She and Paul had one more week of their honeymoon and Mac had apparently returned to Washington. All vestiges of that day had been removed from the Grier house and Cinnamon had disposed of the wilted bouquet.

She approached Amanda's Bridal and Tuxedo Shoppe. The gown in the window was gorgeous, a white dress with Belgian lace. Cinnamon thought of the purple gown in her closet, the one that had caused such a problem. It was just as beautiful in its own way, but it would remain there. Wesley Garner had called that morning and broken their date. He wasn't going to be able to escort her to the party in Boston. He was being transferred to a job in England and would be gone before Mary Ellen's party. Cinnamon was disappointed but wished him well.

"Cinnamon."

She heard her name and turned around. "Hello, Amanda."

"I wanted to tell you how sorry I am for the dress mix-up."

"Don't worry about it," Cinnamon said. She hoped that every time she saw Amanda, the dress shop owner would not apologize for the mix-up. It was over and, hopefully, done with. "I hear you're going to be a local celebrity tonight." Cinnamon changed the subject.

Amanda blushed. "I won't be usurping Mac's seat, but I am a little excited about it."

According to the *Indian Falls Weekly,* a complimentary paper delivered every Thursday, Amanda was to appear on a local cable-television station that night to discuss the state of weddings.

"Are you going to watch?"

"I wouldn't miss it. In fact, several of us have decided to watch it together."

"At Zahara's house?"

"How did you know?"

"She often had the neighbors in. It was just something she did. It became sort of a tradition. I'm surprised people haven't dropped by before this. Maybe with Mac no longer living there, it might be a little awkward."

Cinnamon knew Mac had stayed in the house, but each time someone brought it up, her blood seemed to heat up at the thought of him freely walking through the rooms. She hadn't figured out which bedroom was his, but she was sure she could feel his presence if she went into the extra rooms. Which she hadn't.

"That hasn't kept them away," Cinnamon told the bridal shop owner. "Several of the neighbors have come by to introduce themselves and tell me stories about my grandmother."

"She was a wonder. You'll have to see the collection she donated to the library."

"Library? I haven't heard about that."

"Drop by, it's a great collection."

"I will," Cinnamon promised.

"I am so nervous," Amanda said. "I don't know

how I'm going to be when I'm actually in front of the cameras." She'd reverted back to the previous conversation.

"You'll be fine," Cinnamon assured her.

"I think it'll give the store a boost," Amanda whispered, conspiratorially.

"I'm sure it will."

Cinnamon continued to think that as she waited for Amanda's performance that night. Her television room was full of people. Cinnamon served coffee and the local bakery owner had supplied the pastries. The room was quiet as the program started. The doorbell rang and Cinnamon moved toward it. She didn't know how many people would show up. Fletcher Caton was closer to the door and he opened it.

Cinnamon's mouth dropped when she saw Mac come in. He smiled and shook hands with Fletcher.

"Hey, Mac," Fletcher said. "I wasn't sure you were going to make it this time."

"Traffic was heavy," he said.

Cinnamon stood mute. Mac was the last person she expected. He looked at her with a question in his eyes.

"Come on in," she said hospitably. "The program is just beginning. Can I get you something?"

"Coffee, if you have any."

She'd set up an urn in the dining room. She moved toward it.

"I'll get it," Mac said.

He moved past her, going straight to the machine and getting a cup. Cinnamon thought how he moved quickly and easily to the dining room, as if he'd done it a hundred times.

Cinnamon went back to her seat, which was as far as she could get from him. What was he doing here? Wasn't he supposed to be in D.C.?

The cordial greetings of her neighbors ceased as Amanda was introduced. She smiled from the big screen. Cinnamon glanced at Mac. She seemed drawn to him. Despite what she'd said to Samara, Mac was like a magnet drawing her to him.

Amanda was poised in front of the camera. She answered the questions with only a few "ands" and "uhs." Her audience in the room listened attentively, nodding now and then or agreeing with some of her comments. Time seemed to drag for Cinnamon. She couldn't concentrate. Each time she looked up, she met Mac's eyes. Finally the interview was nearly over. She stared at the television screen, willing herself to listen to Amanda and her host.

"Amanda, you must see and hear many unusual things about weddings," the host said. "People who want to make their day a little different, a bit more special than any of the previous traditions. Could you tell our audience some of the more unique bridal stories that you've helped make a reality?"

"One recent story comes to mind," Amanda said, playing to the camera, and with no hesitation. "This happened to someone who wasn't the bride."

To Cinnamon's horror, Amanda went on to relate the story of the wrong gown. The room laughed at each sentence she finished. Cinnamon would probably be laughing, too, if Mac hadn't been glaring at her. Amanda never mentioned their names, but everyone in the room knew exactly who she meant and thought it was hilarious. When she finished, the group looked from one of them to the other as if they were at a tennis match watching a ball being volleyed back and forth.

Whatever the host said to end the program, Cinnamon never heard. Several minutes later, her guests began to drift out. Most were still laughing as they filed out the door. Mac wasn't laughing and he wasn't leaving. She wondered why until the two of them were alone in the room.

"You think this is funny?" Mac began.

"Don't you have someplace to be?" Cinnamon picked up several cups and headed for the kitchen.

"Not at the present." Mac grabbed a few cups and followed her.

"Yes, I think there is some humor in it. Otherwise those people who just left should be committed." She went back to the dining room and returned with a stack of saucers.

"This is *not* funny," Mac emphasized. "I have a reputation to maintain and I don't like being described as a raving lunatic."

"I don't think Amanda mentioned raving." Cinnamon was enjoying his discomfort.

Mac stepped in front of her as she tried to leave the kitchen.

"Mac, let it go. It's a cable station in a town with less than 3,500 people. The airwaves aren't strong enough to reach the nation's capital. Your secret is safe."

He seemed to understand. His shoulders dropped. "Maybe I am blowing this up a little."

"Not used to being the butt of the joke?" She moved around him and retrieved more dishes. Cinnamon understood that position all too well. In Boston she was often on the receiving end of someone's practical joke or snide remark. But she'd learned to laugh at a lot of them. If she didn't, they would continue and get worse.

Mac was stacking dishes in the dishwasher when she came back. "You don't have to do that," she said.

He glanced at the dishwasher. "I used to do this when I lived here."

Cinnamon put the dishes down. She felt as if she were going to drop them. "I forgot. You did used to live here. Why?"

"Why did I live here?"

Cinnamon nodded.

Mac turned back to the dishwasher and continued stacking the saucers. "The official answer is I needed a quiet place to work when I was here."

"And the unofficial answer?"

"Do you have any food? I haven't had anything to eat since lunch."

Cinnamon had made a meatloaf for dinner. She went to the refrigerator and took it out. In minutes, he was seated at the table with a plate of her leftover meal.

"Aren't you having any?"

"I've already eaten and had some pastry." She glanced toward the dining room which still held a decent amount of pastries.

"Now, the unofficial answer as to why I lived here is that Paul and my sister were constantly together. They didn't actually live together in the beginning. But more and more he was there. They made a lot of noise, laughing, talking. It was hard to concentrate. I felt like a fifth wheel. Zahara allowed me to use a room here. When I worked late into the night, I'd fall asleep on the bed in the room next to yours. When Zahara gave me a room here, Paul took to staying with Allison."

Cinnamon nearly gasped at the room he mentioned.

"One morning when I came down, she made me breakfast and left a door key next to my plate. Zahara said it was for when I needed it."

"And you never left?"

"I left after the will was read."

There was silence for a long moment. Mac finished his food and got up to refill his coffee cup. Cinnamon felt as if her presence had evicted him. It was irrational, but she couldn't help it.

"What do you want with the house?"

"I like it. It's part of the history of this town and I like the town."

"Don't you have a home in D.C.?"

"Georgetown," he said, nodding and resuming his seat. "A very impressive address. It's where I work, where I entertain. Indian Falls is where I live. With Allison and Paul starting out, they need time to be alone and eventually they will start a family."

"Don't you both own the house?"

He nodded. "We did. My interest in it was my wedding present to them. It's totally converted for Allison's needs."

He didn't need to justify his action. Cinnamon thought it was a wonderful thing to do. Much like Samara had done for her. Their grandmother had left the house to Cinnamon, but she'd offered Samara an interest. Her sister refused, saying she'd stayed in Indian Falls before. She liked living in the District and didn't want to be in a small town.

"That was a wonderful thing to do. I'm sure Allison appreciates it."

He took his plate to the sink, rinsed it and put it in the dishwasher.

"Thank you. I haven't had a home-cooked meal in a while."

"Can't you cook?" From the comfort he'd displayed in the kitchen, she thought he'd have no problem making a meal.

"I can, but food tastes so much better when someone else cooks it. And I'd forgotten how much I like meatloaf."

Cinnamon hadn't had it in a long time. Being in front of a television camera had ingrained in her the need to watch her weight. She usually went for salads and fruit.

"So what are you doing here now?" Cinnamon asked. "Since you no longer own the house."

"I have a few things to pick up while Allison is away. And I wanted to see Amanda's debut as a television star."

"And now? After her anecdote?" Cinnamon laughed when she recalled Amanda's rendition of Mac's anger over her wearing the wedding gown.

When she looked at him, she expected to see either humor or anger, but neither expression was on his face. His stare was intense, heated, and Cinnamon suddenly thought they were no longer talking about the same thing.

After an eternity, he stood up. "I'd better go."

She stood and together they headed for the front door. At the door, neither of them reached to open it.

"I suppose I won't be seeing you again," Cinnamon said. The thought of it made her a little sad. She didn't know why. "That is unless I meet my sister for lunch."

"Yeah," he smiled.

"Well, good night," she said a little awkwardly. Both of them reached for the knob at the same time. Their fingers touched and caught. She looked at their hands, locked together like chains for several moments. Then she looked up at him. All she could see in his eyes were questions. Cinnamon didn't understand them.

After a moment, Mac dropped her hand and pulled the door inward. Without a word, he went out into the night. Cinnamon closed the door and headed back to the kitchen. There were still the pastries to wrap up and the dishwasher to run, and the television room needed straightening. But somewhere between the door and the kitchen, Cinnamon stopped.

"What was that?" she asked herself. Her mind had refused to process her holding hands with Mac. Or him with her. Didn't they dislike each other? Then why had they talked so easily in the kitchen? And why did she feel that there was something more in store for them?

Suddenly, she shook her head, jarring herself back to reality. She was off men and that included MacKenzie Grier. She told herself that. But could she remember her vow the next time she saw him?

Anyone who wanted a good meal in Indian Falls had to go to Velma's. She owned and operated the only restaurant in town. Mac turned into the parking lot the next morning and noticed the place was doing a good business. Cars were three deep, and he squeezed in between a Camry and a super Escalade.

Velma's restaurant was like a local bar for the morning crowd. Everyone met there for both conversation and good food. Mac was sure the general talk this morning would be Amanda's appearance on television the night before. He wasn't disappointed. The moment he opened the door he was greeted with "what did you think of Amanda?" Of course, this was accompanied with a bit of good-natured laughter. Although Mac didn't see it that way. He wasn't a joker.

Allison had left very little food in the house since she and Paul would be away for two weeks. Mac hadn't decided how long he was going to stay, so he hadn't brought anything with him. He thought of the meatloaf he'd eaten last night at Cinnamon's. She was a good cook, making even a simple meal feel both substantial and elegant.

At his sister's, the quiet afforded him time to get some much needed work done, but of late each time he passed the city limit, his thoughts immediately flew to the town's newest resident. That's where it had been this morning when he woke. And now as he took a seat in the restaurant, the town also put them together.

Mac usually sat at the counter when he was

alone, but every seat was occupied when he entered the place. A couple got up to leave as he made his way to the end of the room and he took their table.

"Morning, Mac, what can I get you?" Velma asked, as she cleaned the table. Mac had known her for as long as he could remember. She rarely waited tables anymore. She had a full staff, but this morning the place was unusually busy and apparently all hands were needed.

"The full American," he said. It was the specialty of the house, included everything: coffee, juice, eggs, various breads, sausage, bacon and the staple of the South—grits. Even though he'd had a big dinner at Cinnamon's, he was famished this morning.

Velma poured his coffee and smiled as she left him. Velma heard everything and knew everything going on in the small hamlet, but she wasn't one to spread gossip. The other citizens of Indian Falls gathered and talked, speculated and laughed over the crisis of the moment, but Velma knew how to keep hold on what she knew.

Mac tried to concentrate on his newspaper while he waited, but people kept stopping by or talking to him from other tables. Indian Falls was that kind of place. And Velma's was that kind of place, too. Neighbors were friendly and always

willing to stop and talk. Velma poured him a
second cup as he went back to his paper. He
accepted it without looking up. With the hot liquid
halfway to his mouth, he heard his name. Lilly,
one of the young waitresses, was standing near the
door and pointing in his direction. Next to her was
Zahara Lewis's granddaughter. Mac's throat
closed off and he set the cup back in its saucer.
Cinnamon circuited the tables, weaving back and
forth as she searched for a place to sit. Mac had a
table for two and one of the chairs was empty.

Cinnamon didn't appear to want to sit with him.
She looked everywhere but in his direction. He
stood up as she neared him.

"If you're looking for a seat, I'm willing to share."

Mac noticed the noise level had decreased in the
room and several of the patrons were openly
staring at them. Cinnamon looked around.

"I don't want to disturb you," she said.

"There aren't any other seats," Mac pointed out.
He pulled out the chair and she sat down. Despite
the busy room, Velma and the waitresses moved
about like a well-practiced dance team. Velma
appeared with the coffee pot and at Cinnamon's
nod, filled her cup.

"The full American is the specialty of the house,"
Mac told her. "I can vouch for it."

"All right." She gave the order to Velma.

"I don't mean to impose," she told Mac. "You can go on with what you were doing. Pretend I'm not here."

"I don't think that's possible," Mac said.

"Was that a compliment?"

Mac shrugged. "Even if I wanted to ignore you, I don't think the crowd would allow it."

Cinnamon looked around. People were glancing covertly at them. She was glad when Velma set plates in front of them and went on to fill the small table with toast, butter, pastries, condiments and baskets of jams, jellies and preserves.

Cinnamon's eyes opened wide when she saw everything. "I didn't know what a full order an American was," she said. "With all this, I may still be here when Allison and Paul return."

Mac dug in. He didn't want to discuss the wedding.

"Will you be here until they return?" she asked conversationally.

"I haven't decided. I could get a lot of work done without a lot of interruptions."

"I hated to see all the decorations come down," Cinnamon began. "The house looked so festive with the decorated tables and flowers. But I guess you can't have a wedding every day."

"No, you can't," he said flatly.

Cinnamon took a bite of her eggs. "May I ask you a personal question?"

Mac stopped eating and folded his hands, elbows on the table. He stared at Cinnamon. He was sure he knew what she was going to ask. "What do you want to know?"

"At the wedding. You looked very…uncomfortable. I mean even when you weren't looking at me. Don't you like Paul? Is he not good enough for your sister?"

He relaxed. "I think Paul is perfect for my sister. He worships the ground she rolls over."

Cinnamon smiled a moment, but didn't give up on an answer to her question. Mac didn't want to tell her the real reason. He hated reviewing that humiliating day. But he supposed she'd hear the enhanced version if he didn't give her the true facts.

"I suppose you haven't heard about my wedding."

Her eyes opened wide and she sat back. "I didn't know you were married."

"I'm not. Never have been."

"Oh."

Her face showed him she was more confused now than before.

"If you stay around here a while, you'll hear the story." He paused. "She left me standing at the altar."

Cinnamon gasped. "You're kidding?"

"I wish I was. It was humiliating, so I don't like weddings, don't want anything to do with them."

"How did you get out of the church?"

Mac remembered the anger that came over him when he realized he was going to have to announce to the congregation that there would be no wedding.

"It's mainly a blur. The bride's father came back and gave me the letter. The minister offered to let the guests know, but I went out, told them there would be no wedding. The other three men were with me."

"Mac, I'm sorry. That's an awful thing to do to a person."

"I've survived it." He shrugged.

"This is a small town, a place where people have long memories. It must have been hard to walk the streets after that."

"As luck would have it, the wedding wasn't here, but there were enough people from Indian Falls attending, including Zahara. The sorrowful looks are gone and no one mentions it to me anymore."

"But you know they're thinking it?"

He nodded. "Every time someone gets engaged or has an anniversary. If I never attend another wedding, it would be fine with me."

"But as Allison's brother, you were forced to be in her wedding."

He smiled quickly. "She manipulated me at every turn. And I knew it. I was relieved when it was over and everything went off fine."

"Did you doubt that Paul would show up?"

He shook his head. "I was the best man. It was my job to get him to the church. Paul was a little nervous, but he wanted to marry Allison. He just wanted the ceremony behind him. Paul's not one to be at the center of attention."

"What was her name?" Cinnamon asked.

Mac knew who she meant. "Jerrilyn McGowan. She lives in San Francisco now."

"Mac, I'm sorry." She reached across the table and put her hand on his. Mac was immediately aware of the softness of her touch, but there was also a live wire inside the gentleness of it. "I can see why you don't want anything to do with weddings."

"It's all right. I've had two years to get used to it. But I'm not that lucky. There is still another wedding I'm obligated to attend. My best friend's. I'm standing up for him, too." He hoped she didn't hear the reluctance in his voice.

"Cinnamon, there you are." A happy voice called them. Fletcher Caton was making his way toward their table. He grabbed an empty chair from a table someone was vacating and pulled it up next to them.

"Morning, Mac," he said.

"Fletcher," Mac acknowledged. "Who's watching the store?" Fletcher was rarely away from the gift shop during working hours. He watched over it like it was his child.

"I put the sign out," he said.

That meant he closed it until he could get back.

"I had an epiphany," Fletcher said, looking at Cinnamon.

"An epiphany about what?" Cinnamon asked.

"Your wedding."

"*My* wedding. I'm not getting married."

"Let me explain," Fletcher said. "After watching Amanda last night, I thought it would be a good idea to give away free invitations to a wedding."

Cinnamon looked questioningly at Mac. He didn't know where Fletcher was going with this.

"It's a business ploy, I admit that." Fletcher looked a little shy, but recovered quickly. "I'm willing to provide you with top-of-the-line invitations for your wedding as long as it's all right with you if I advertise the invitations in the local paper."

"But, Fletcher, I'm not even engaged to anyone. You can't have an invitation with Groom: TBA written on it."

Mac laughed at that. Cinnamon looked at him for help, but he had none to give.

"Well, I'm sure wedding bells will soon ring for you, too. You caught the bouquet."

"You can't believe that really means anything."

"Allison Grier must have. She flung it straight at you." He swung his gaze from Cinnamon to Mac and back again.

"She did," Cinnamon acknowledged, but added nothing more.

"Fletcher, how do you think this will help your business?" Mac asked.

"Everyone loves a wedding, except you, Mac." He glanced again from one to the other, then back to Cinnamon. "You're Zahara's granddaughter and you're living in her house. If I give invitations to you, others will do business at my store."

"My grandmother had that much influence?"

"She was the Oprah of Indian Falls. If she recommended something, it sold like hotcakes."

"Fletcher, I have no problem with you giving me invitations, if and when I get engaged, but right now the groom is still TBA."

Cinnamon laughed as Fletcher left. He was happy, threading his way through the crowd before going out of the restaurant and back toward his shop.

"Where does he get these ideas?" she asked.

"It was an epiphany," Mac answered.

Chapter 5

"Cinnamon, what is going on down there? You're on the front page of *The Weekly*."

"Is it a good picture?" Cinnamon yawned into the phone.

"This is not a joke," Samara scolded.

"Only if you don't laugh at it. What are you doing with *The Weekly* anyway?" *The Weekly* was the *Indian Falls Weekly*, a local paper that had been published continuously for the past seventy-five years.

"I have a subscription," she answered.

Cinnamon pushed herself up in the bed.

"Are you still sleeping? Don't tell me you're still in bed."

"Samara, what are you so upset about?"

"Me! I'm not upset, but you should be. You wanted to be taken seriously down there. How do you think this will play at the weather station when you start work?"

"How do I think what will play?"

"Cinnamon, you have read the paper?"

She could hear the censure in her sister's voice. "I've been a little busy and that paper never has anything in it other than how many jars of preserves Minnie Wilson is donating to the county fair."

"Well, they've come up in the world and your wedding invitation is on the front page."

"*What* wedding invitation?" Cinnamon carried the portable phone with her as she ran downstairs to the stack of unread letters and papers she needed to respond to. She ripped the paper from its plastic bag and turned it to page one. There was her photo, one that had been taken at Allison's wedding. Someone had snapped that photo when Mac had asked her dance.

"Oh no," she said. On the front page was a copy of the invitation with her name as bride and Groom: TBA written in bold letters. Cinnamon started to laugh.

"You think this is funny?" Samara said.

"Of course, it's funny. What else could it be? Obviously, this is a joke, Samara."

Cinnamon thought of Fletcher leaving the restaurant. His step was lively, as if he'd gotten what he wanted. And then she remembered seeing someone follow him out. At the time she hadn't though anything of it. After all, Mac was distracting her. Now she remembered who it was—Sonia Archer, reporter for *The Indian Falls Weekly*. Cinnamon wondered how much of Fletcher's conversation she'd heard.

"Cinnamon, are you still there?"

"I'm here. Samara, this is nothing. It was a marketing program that Fletcher wanted to run." She went on to explain the breakfast meeting and seeing Sonia leave right after Fletcher.

"As I said, this is not the way to start a new job."

"I don't think anyone will care about this. It's a joke. Fletcher offered me some invitations. I refused them."

"And you made the front page with that refusal."

Cinnamon wished Samara would stop saying that.

The story didn't call for righteous indignation, Cinnamon thought as she dressed and prepared to confront Fletcher Caton, at least not at the level

Samara thought it should. Cinnamon walked briskly along the street, heading for Fletcher's gift shop. She wasn't a mail-order bride. She wasn't a bride by proxy. She wasn't even a jilted bride. But mostly she wasn't a *bride* at all. And, as a non-bride, she didn't need invitations.

Fletcher's shop sold an assortment of unique items, from greeting cards to Swarovski Crystal. Some of the *objets d'art* were hard to find in other places. They were so beautiful and different.

"Fletcher, what is this?" she asked, opening the newspaper as she entered his shop. Thankfully, the place was empty.

He smiled broadly as if nothing out of the ordinary had happened.

"You know I'm not engaged. How could you put this in the paper? And without telling me."

"I promise, I didn't know Sonia was going to write that up."

"Fletcher, she's a reporter. What did you think she would do?"

"I thought she'd give me some free advertising. Maybe a few people from the highway would stop in on their way to or from home. Maybe they would buy a few things."

"People, like from, say Boston." She gave him her best smile.

"Them, too," he agreed, scratching his head a little nervously.

"And that's why it states prominently that I am a former TV personality from WBSN in Boston." She should be glad she wasn't referred to as a weather girl. "And there's nothing about me being employed with the National Weather Service in a very well-respected position."

"That's probably because the story is about the invitations we provide."

"Then why is my name on it and the catch phrase, Groom: TBA?"

He tried not to smile, but the corners of his lips turned up. "It was too good a phrase to bypass. And the offer is still open. You find a man to put on that invitation and I'll make up as many as you need—no charge."

He raised his hands and shook his head at the same time. The bell above the door rang and Fletcher immediately left her to take care of his customer. Cinnamon stood there several moments. In the background she could hear the muted sound of Fletcher's voice transacting a sale.

The humor of the situation hit her again. A bubble of laughter caught in her throat and she tried to hold it, but she couldn't. Soon she was smiling. She put her hand up to cover her mouth and turned to leave.

Mac stood behind her. He had a small box in his hand which he put in his pocket. She hadn't seen him come in the store, but there were several people browsing now.

"I suppose that newspaper article strikes you as laughable, too," he said, looking down at the paper she had left on the counter.

"Yes," she giggled. "It does. It would be even funnier if we put your name next to the word *groom*. Shall I call Fletcher and give him—"

His face went dark. "Don't even joke about that," he interrupted. His body tightened. Everything about him seemed to recoil. His hands grabbed her upper arms.

"Mac." She wiggled herself free of his grip. "Give it a rest. It was just a joke."

"You know how I feel about weddings. I don't joke about them."

"I suppose you got up on the wrong side of the bed this morning. Writing not going well?"

"As a matter of fact, it isn't. I guess I got too used to writing at Zahara's."

Cinnamon stiffened. That was not going to happen again. She was not that neighborly. He could not use a room in her house. It might help his writing, but it would destroy her peace of mind. Each time she saw him, her heartbeat increased and she wouldn't even think what would happen to her blood pressure with him in the house.

"I thought your show was off the cuff. What are you writing?"

"The discussion is spontaneous, but I have to ask questions, know the backgrounds and history of the subject."

"So you're writing notes?"

"Not exactly. While the show might look spontaneous, it's well coordinated and I'm one of the writers."

"I'm sure you'll find your inspiration soon and the words will flow fast and furiously." She wasn't even going to entertain the obvious solution to his dilemma. It was his problem, not hers. She wasn't going to get into it. "Excuse me, I have to go now." Cinnamon started for the door, passing Fletcher as she went out onto the street.

She'd been walking fast, but Mac caught up with her ten feet from the door.

"You seem in an awful hurry."

"I am. I have a few things to pick up and I need to pack." Cinnamon was in a hurry for another reason. Mac threw her equilibrium off. Even with his hands hard on her arms, she felt the tingle of arousal.

"Leaving so soon? You haven't decided to sell, have you?"

"Don't you wish?"

"Actually, no."

His tone caught her attention and she looked up into his eyes. They were beautiful, dark-brown with the hint of a secret hidden in their depths. Cinnamon nearly swayed toward him.

"Where are you going?"

An idea came to her suddenly. So suddenly that she nearly discarded it before she let it form. She stared at Mac. He was good-looking. Not as gorgeous as Wesley Garner. But as eye candy, both men fit the bill.

"Cinnamon?"

"Mac, what are you doing this weekend?" The question came out in a rush. Almost as if she had to get it out before her courage deserted her.

"What?"

"This weekend. You said your writing isn't going well. Do you think you can put it off until Monday?"

"Are you asking me out?"

She nodded. There was a bubble in her throat that refused to let her speak.

"Why?" Mac stood back and eyed her skeptically.

"I want you to go somewhere with me," she said.

"Where?"

"To a party."

"As what?"

"My date."

"You're kidding, right? This is one of your jokes."

"No joke. I'm serious."

"Why would you want to date me? I'm sure you have no problem getting dates."

Mac was not only handsome. He was delicious to look at, if she let herself think about his physical attributes. Which she wouldn't. But he could help her out this weekend.

"I need a date and you're free."

"A date for what?"

"A party. The one I bought the dress for."

He seemed to frown when she mentioned the dress. They both remembered clashing over Allison's gown. But the dress Cinnamon was planning to wear was the one the delivery man should have brought.

"The party is in Boston," she blurted out.

"You're asking me to go away for the weekend?"

Cinnamon looked around. They were standing on a public street. She didn't want people staring at them. There was no one around and she was too far from Fletcher's store to see through the glass windows.

"Don't make it sound like I'm asking you to go to a wedding." Cinnamon knew asking him was a bad idea. What had made her do it? She wasn't usually so impulsive. "You know what? Let's forget it. It was a bad idea. I should never have asked."

She turned and walked away. She felt like an idiot. Why had she done something so utterly stupid?

"I'll go," he said, catching up with her.

"Don't bother. It wasn't a good idea." She continued walking. "I should never have brought it up."

"I'll go," he said again. "I want to go."

"You do?" She stopped and looked at him.

"Why don't you tell me about it?"

"It's the—"

"Not here." He stopped her. "My house isn't far. Why don't we go there? I'll make you a latte."

He casually took her arm and Cinnamon felt the solidity of his hand. She didn't want him to let go. Moments later they were sitting on opposite sides of a low table on the back porch of his house, lattes in front of them.

The house that Allison and Paul would occupy was closer to town than Cinnamon's house. The porch was really a covered veranda that had been updated a few years earlier, Samara had told her. It held an outdoor fireplace used to warm the cool nights and extend the summer a few more weeks.

"Who's giving the party?" he asked.

"My friend, Mary Ellen. Mary Ellen Taylor. I've known her since college. She gives an annual Start of the Summer Ball. And it's this weekend."

"Black tie, I suppose."

"Don't you have a tux?" She frowned. The event was a ball. Everyone dressed.

"I'm sure I can scare one up," he said, taking a sip from his cup.

"What happened to your date?"

"How did you know I had a date?"

The look he gave her said someone who looked like her wouldn't be going to a ball alone. "He got transferred to England."

"Ah, the ole transferred to England story." He gave her the slippery eel smile. Cinnamon couldn't help laughing.

"He really did get transferred."

"Oh, I believe you. It's his loss, my gain."

Mac was confusing Cinnamon. What did he mean his *gain?* He didn't like her; the two had been oil and water since they'd met. She discounted the feelings that she suppressed when he was around. She'd been in his arms, dancing with him, knew the sound of his heart beating. But he'd never given her an inkling that he had any feelings for her.

There was the meatloaf night. They'd talked like

friends and there was that one moment when she felt that Mac had wanted to kiss her. But it had been lost quickly. Now she didn't know what to think.

"So, give me some details other than I need a tux," he said.

"There isn't much. It's a party. It'll be at Mary Ellen's parents' house in Cambridge. The place will be filled with Boston society and some plain ole folks. You'll be fine. It'll be nothing like a wedding."

She watched him recede again.

"Is that a word we're not going to be able to say around you? You know you can't hide from it. It happens too often."

"No, it's not a removed-from-the-dictionary word."

"Then you have to stop reacting to it."

"I'm not reacting to the word."

"Then what is it? Every time someone says *wedding,* your teeth clamp together and your jaws are so tight you could break a tooth."

"Good metaphor," he said and gave her a quick smile. Cinnamon liked his smile. It did funny things to her stomach. "At this party, who am I? I mean who am I to you?"

"My date."

"Nothing more?"

She thought about that for a moment. She did want him to be more. The thought struck her like being hit with a club. But she forced herself not to change her expression.

"Nothing more," she said.

"Just checking."

"You know, you don't have to do this." She wasn't feeling so good about her invitation now. Impulsiveness was never a good idea. "In fact, I think I'll just rescind the invitation."

"Not on your life. If you don't take me with you, I'll go to Boston and find Mary Ellen Taylor and tell her how you stole the bride's gown and then crashed her wedding."

There, he'd said it. She knew he did it to let her know the word didn't frighten him.

"She'll laugh. The same as I would."

"Well, you still don't have a date. And I'm available." He turned slightly away from her and looked at the sky, patting his foot as if waiting for her to cave.

Cinnamon laughed. "All right. We leave Friday at noon. The party is Saturday night. We come back Sunday. Can you manage that?"

He got up and walked to the fireplace. "Where are we staying?"

"My house."

"You have a house in Boston?"

"Actually, it's my mother's house. She's away on one of those Alaskan cruises with my aunt. Then the two of them are going to spend a couple of weeks in Seattle visiting their other sister before returning."

"Sounds like fun."

She wasn't sure if he meant her mother and her sisters or the two of them having the house alone.

"Don't get any ideas. You get a room and a bed. Nothing more."

"Not even breakfast?"

"There's an IHOP close by. I'll even spring for it."

"No," he disagreed. "Breakfast will be on me."

"I have to go and get some things done," she began. "I'll see you on Friday."

"Not so fast." He stopped her. "I have a condition. I do you a favor, you do one for me."

Cinnamon sat back down. "What is it?"

Mac took a breath and waited a moment. She wondered what condition he could impose.

"It's about a wedding."

"What about a wedding?"

"I need a date, too."

"You want me to go a wedding with you?"

He was back to looking as if he'd rather have his fingernails removed.

"If I could have gotten out of it, I would have."

"You don't look like you'd have a problem getting a date to a wedding." She deliberately said the *W* word, throwing him the same argument he'd given her.

"I need someone who won't expect any entanglements after it's over."

"And that would be me?" She lowered her chin and looked at him with hard eyes.

"That would be you." He hesitated a moment. "I know that came out wrong, but I need a date for a wedding and since you don't really like me, you'd be perfect."

"I get it," Cinnamon said. It dawned on her that he needed to use her for something. "Which is it, you're trying to circumvent a previous relationship or someone is trying to set you up and you want to thwart their plans?"

"The first."

He'd answered immediately. At least he was honest. Cinnamon liked that about him. Her face softened a little.

"She's my ex-fiancée. She'll be at the wedding."

"Exactly what role am I supposed to play?"

He looked confused a second before a light seemed to dawn in his brain. "Oh, you won't need to play the loving girlfriend."

"But I'm more than, say, a buddy?" She spread her hands. "More than, maybe, a sister figure?" She stared steadily at him. "Maybe it's a first date kind of thing." She got up and crossed the space to where he stood. "I smile a lot, make polite conversation with your friends." She moved around him, lowering her voice. "But I don't hang on your arm like this." She took his arm, slipped hers through it and pressed her shoulder against his. "I don't curve myself around you." She demonstrated her words. "And continually offer my mouth for a kiss."

She was close enough for their mouths to touch. He stared down at her lips, saying nothing. Cinnamon felt the warmth of his mouth, tasted the latte he'd drunk across the small space separating them. She'd discovered she hadn't thought this ploy through. She wanted him to kiss her. In a moment, she'd remove that tiny distance and do what she wanted to do. He'd kissed her before and she wanted him to do it again.

"Be careful, Cinnamon, you're no longer on solid ground."

For a moment Cinnamon hung where she was. She liked the solid feel of him more than she should. Suddenly, she moved back. Then walked across to the railing and looked out over the yard that had so recently held huge round tables and been crowded with guests.

"Yeah," she finally said. "Going to a wedding with someone you don't really like appears to be the perfect solution." She turned around, keeping the distance between them. Her body felt wet, like she needed a shower—a cold shower. "Who's getting married?" she asked, hoping her voice sounded normal.

"My best friend. I'm the best man so I have to be there. But it's not for another month."

"I like weddings. I want to have a huge one, white dress with all the trimmings."

"Just like Allison's."

She nodded. "I've dreamed of it all my life."

"Are you doing anything to make it happen?" He looked at her inquiringly. "Just because you don't have a date for this party doesn't mean you don't have a line of suitors."

"If you're asking if there's a man in my life, not at the moment."

"Good, I'd hate to run into someone who misunderstands our *date*."

Mac was old enough to recognize that there were cycles in the lives of every circle of friends. There was the cycle when they all graduated high

school and went off to college. Then the cycle
when they began their first jobs. Now there was the
marriage cycle. He looked down at the third invitation he'd received this year for the wedding of
one of his friends. Not to mention his own sister's
wedding just a week ago. In a year or two there
would be the baby cycle.

Mac placed the dishes in the dishwasher after
Cinnamon left. He frowned at the thought of going
away with her. He had to be out of his mind. What
had possessed him to say he'd go with her? And
say it more than once.

His briefcase sat open on the kitchen table. He
lifted the envelope on top of the papers and pulled
the single card out. Mr. and Mrs. Adam Tate request
the honor of your presence at the nuptials of their
daughter Sandra Marie to Mr. Richard Briscoe.
Mac read the gold lettering on the cream-colored
card stock. He'd known Rick since they were kids.
Rick had escaped Indian Falls and gone to D.C.,
where he was now to be married. Mac couldn't
stop the frown. Every wedding reminded him of his
own. At least the one he'd almost had. And along
with that came the humiliating way it had ended.

Mac sat down, still holding the invitation.
Jerrilyn was in San Francisco. She'd moved there
right after the havoc she'd created in D.C., leaving

him to clean up her mess. Rick knew them both.
So did his fiancée, Sandra, who was friends with
Jerrilyn. It was impossible to think that Jerrilyn
wasn't reading a similar invitation to the same
wedding. He had to go. Rick had been his friend
since life began and Mac was the best man. But he
didn't look forward to seeing the woman he'd been
engaged to marry again, especially in a setting that
called for white gowns, tuxedos and 'til death do
us part. He'd been to three weddings this year
alone and she had been at every one of them. While
she'd come with a date, he'd gone stag. Not this
time.

Pulling the reply card forward, Mac looked at
the blank line requesting the number in his party.
Without hesitation he grabbed a pen and with sure
and bold strokes wrote the number two. Twenty-
four hours ago he hadn't the slightest idea who
number two would be, but he sure as hell wasn't
going alone.

Now, out of the blue, he had a date. Immediately her face came into his mind.

Cinnamon Scott. Mac smiled. She was beautiful, poised and could hold her own. She held it
with him. And he was no pushover. Cinnamon
would give Jerrilyn a run for her money.

Mac suddenly felt good. Really good.

Chapter 6

The house in Boston reflected the difference between her mother's world and that of her father. And now that she'd been living in Zahara Lewis's house for nearly a month, Cinnamon understood more why her parents' lives would never mesh in a marriage.

Her mother's home was modern. The house was one of the old brownstones of Boston, near enough to Copley Square for a good walk and far enough away to give it an old neighborhood feel. But that was the only thing old about it. The inside had been gutted and redone several times. Now the place had an open feel to it that let the light in and was decorated with bold colors and plush furniture.

Cinnamon had had her own apartment when she lived in Boston. Her hours were strange and she wanted to be on her own. Her mother hadn't objected. She said she understood and the two had never been enemies. The only subject they disagreed on was Cinnamon's father's family. Although her mother was tolerant of Samara, she'd kept Cinnamon away from her father's family as much as possible. That was why she rarely visited her grandmother. When Zahara had bequeathed her the house, it had been a total surprise, but it was timely.

Cinnamon led Mac upstairs to the bedrooms. Only in Cinnamon's room was there traditional furniture. She opened the door at the end of the hall where Mac would sleep. It had a modern fireplace, a platform bed and mirrored drawers on the dressers. One wall had been painted electric blue. The other walls were a soft robin's egg blue and everything else was white, from the carpet to the bedcovers. Throw pillows picked up the contrasting wall colors.

Mac turned totally around. His suit bag and suitcase were still in his hands. "No mirrors on the ceiling?" he asked.

"I drew the line there," Cinnamon said. "My mother is rather extreme."

"What does your room look like?"

"Very traditional, but you don't need to see it." She stopped him immediately.

"Don't worry. I wasn't angling for an invitation."

"This is the calmest guest room in the house. Believe me, the others are, shall we say, more colorful."

Mac put his suitcase down.

"I'll leave you to settle in."

"Hey." He stopped her. "What are we doing tonight?"

Cinnamon stammered. She hadn't thought of doing anything. "Nothing in particular. I thought I'd stay in, wash my hair. But don't let me keep you. If you want to go out, I can give you a key."

"It's early. Why don't I wash your hair and we could go out to dinner later tonight?"

Images of them naked in the shower, shampoo lather dripping from her hair while Mac's hands covered the rest of her body had her tingling with anticipation. But she knew better.

"Why don't *I* wash my hair? And we can get something to eat later."

"You don't trust me with shampoo and water?"

"In a word, no," Cinnamon said. Yet it wasn't Mac she didn't trust. She could still feel his mouth on hers. The idea of his hands rhythmically massaging her scalp with her being in a virtually helpless position, was something she thought she should avoid.

"You don't know what you're missing," he said. "I'm very good."

"Don't tell me, somewhere in your past you were a shampoo clerk?"

"No, I'd just like to get my hands in your hair."

Heat slammed into Cinnamon as if she'd opened a hot oven. "Whatever happened to 'we don't like each other'?" she asked.

"I thought I'd put it on hold for the weekend."

Cinnamon smiled. "I approve of that. It'll make the party a lot more fun."

"Not to mention the rest of the weekend."

Cinnamon didn't understand what was happening to her. It seemed to happen each time she was in Mac's presence. And being in a bedroom alone with him was the *wrong* setting. She took a step back.

"I'll make a reservation," Mac said. He, too, moved a step away from her. Cinnamon wondered if he felt the need to break the invisible connection that seemed to pull them together. "What would you like to eat?"

"Seafood." She grabbed onto the ordinary topic of dinner, relieved that whatever was between them had snapped. "Try Docksides or The Sandpiper. The food is excellent at both."

"The Sandpiper is a seafood restaurant?"

"Named after its original owner, Granville Sandpiper. He was a fisherman until he decided to try the land for a while. Bored with inactivity, he opened a restaurant. That was seventy years ago. It's still owned by the family."

Mac nodded.

Cinnamon went to her room and threw the windows open. The wind burst inside. She'd forgotten how much she loved the flow of the breeze. For a moment she let it trail over her face, taking deep breaths and remembering living here. Although she hadn't been gone that long, she'd given up her apartment and only spoke to her friends through e-mail or the phone. It wasn't like they could meet after work for a quick drink. Not that she could do that anyway. She'd been in front of the camera at six and eleven. Drinking in between appearances wasn't a good idea and by the time she was free for the night, most of her friends were asleep. But she'd lived a pleasant life in Boston except for the wisecracks, bad jokes and glass ceiling she'd faced in the weather room.

But that was behind her. Pushing herself back from the breeze, she turned toward the room. She no longer had to deal with any of that. Quickly, she unpacked and stepped under the shower. She was humming to herself, smiling at nothing. Then she realized she was thinking of Mac.

Vigorously she washed her hair. She wondered what he thought of her mother's house. The place took some getting used to. Her friends in high school used to love to come over. Bold colors were in then and their parents were much too conservative to allow them to have purple walls and furniture that was just fun. While Cinnamon never went in for that, preferring traditional furniture, she liked her mother's expression of self. She said her home should reflect who she was and she was a happy, colorful individual.

And she had a totally pink room. Cinnamon laughed. Wait until Mac saw it. She was saving that for later.

With the length of her hair and the fact that it held water like a dam, it took her nearly two hours to complete the process. Dressed in jeans and a Harvard University T-shirt, Cinnamon left the bedroom and headed downstairs.

She didn't know where Mac was. She didn't hear any sound coming from his room, but it was at the opposite end of the hall from hers. She'd purposely put him as far from her as she could get him. Downstairs was just as quiet. At the bottom of the steps, she turned toward the kitchen.

"Does it always take you this long to wash your hair?" Mac startled her when he spoke from directly behind her. She turned around in the downstairs hall.

"Did you miss me?" she teased.

"Wow," he said, his eyes opening wide.

"Thank you. I'll take that as meaning I was worth the wait." She tossed her head and pushed her fingers through her hair.

"You know you're going to have to stop doing that."

"Doing what?" she asked, feigning innocence. She'd never teased a guy before. With Mac it was fun. And the fact that the events involving her "wedding" were laughable to her, but upsetting for him, just made her want to tease him more.

Starting to walk again, she went to the kitchen and opened the refrigerator. A shelf full of bottled water, bottled juice, a can of coffee and the usual assortment of condiments, looked back at her. On the bottom shelf was a bottle of wine, but nothing to eat. Grabbing a bottle of water, she turned back. "Want something?" she asked Mac, holding up the water.

"Yes," he said in a tone that had her hand stopping in midreach.

They were here alone and while her body seemed to have discovered the chemistry of his even from a distance, Cinnamon was not planning to reduce the space between them. She'd sworn off men while she lived in this town, and her vow extended to Virginia and to the man standing in front of her.

"Why don't we go for a walk?" she said.

Mac took the water, twisted the cap and drained the contents in one long swallow. Cinnamon carried hers with her as they went outside and headed up the street of houses that had been a deep, dark red when originally built. Time and weather had changed them to an unfathomable purple, a color Cinnamon had never seen anywhere else.

"Did you grow up here?" Mac asked.

"You mean in that house with all the color?"

He nodded.

"Yes," Cinnamon answered. "It wasn't always like that. My mother changed it several times. Once we had an art deco look. It was totally black and white, with all these elaborate sconces and lacquered plaques on the walls. I never knew what the place would look like when I got home from school. My mother liked to move the furniture around. But after I started working, I got my own place."

"I take it your mom is a free spirit."

"She's a lot of fun. But she got a daughter like me, old-fashioned, traditional."

"Except in the matter of misdirected wedding gowns."

"Except that," Cinnamon agreed. "And my wardrobe. I tend to wear bright colors." She looked down at her shirt and pants. They weren't the shocking colors she usually wore. "I suppose I get my clothes gene from my mother and my decorating gene from my father and grandmother. I love the house in Indian Falls."

"I do, too," Mac said.

Cinnamon remembered he'd wanted to buy Zahara Lewis's house.

"You should have spent more time there when Zahara was alive."

"I wish I had, but my parents' divorce was bad and my mother refused to allow me any contact with my dad's side of the family."

"That doesn't seem very fair."

"They treated her badly."

"Zahara?" He looked surprised.

"I don't think it was her. Mainly my father's

sisters and aunts. They didn't think she was good enough for him. And knowing how my mother lives, I can believe she wasn't a breath of free air to the genteel folks of Virginia."

Cinnamon turned the corner. Ahead of them were the towering buildings that defined the skyline of Boston. For most people, it was surprising to find it so close. Just around the corner and you were almost upon it. In front of them was a small park with a few benches used for relaxing and taking in the air. Cinnamon walked to one of them and the two sat down.

"It wasn't all my father's relatives," she continued. "My parents lived here, not in Virginia. The marriage broke up for other reasons. I'm sure it had more to do with incompatibility than anything else."

"So has this experience soured you on marriage?"

She eyed him cautiously. He was the one sour on marriage. She wondered if that question had an underlying purpose, since Mac had mentioned it.

"I don't think so. I'm cautious. I mean, when I say 'til death do us part, I want to mean it."

"Did you intend to mean it with the guy who went to England?"

"Wesley Garner? He was strictly…" She stopped, unsure how to go on. Wesley was eye candy, but she didn't want to demean him to someone who didn't know him and didn't know her that well, either. "No," she ended weakly. "We were friends. We both know Mary Ellen and he asked me."

She left out the part about her finding her boyfriend and hopeful fiancé with another woman. Wesley knew about it. Everyone knew. Wesley was between women at the time, as hard as that was to believe, and as friends he'd asked her to the party. Of course, she was a local television personality. She knew that was part of the reason Wesley had asked her, but it didn't matter. She wasn't seeing anyone and she did like him as a friend. There was no reason why she shouldn't go with him.

"So where are we going for dinner?" Cinnamon asked, changing the subject.

"Sandpiper's."

The restaurant was packed. It was Friday night, the start of the weekend and the place was noisy. Mac had asked for a quiet table, so he and Cinnamon sat away from the main path the waiters took as they served food and took care of the diners. It was relatively quiet compared to the other part of the room.

Mac tried not to stare at Cinnamon. She was

beautiful. He told himself that he understood beautiful women, but he couldn't keep from looking at her. She wore a simple black dress with a long bright pink scarf that draped over her shoulder and hung down her back.

They'd ordered and received their food. "How'd you get the name Cinnamon?"

"That's very interesting," she said. "My father gave it to me. I get my coloring from him." She put a forkful of food in her mouth and ate. "The story goes that when he first saw me, he said I was the color of cinnamon and that's what they named me. I'm grateful. I could have been Emma. That was the name they had chosen before I was born."

"You don't look like an Emma." Cinnamon was an unusual name, not exactly exotic, but one that made people look up from whatever they were doing. And then they would see her.

"How did you become MacKenzie?" she asked.

"It's a family name, my grandfather's. He ran a boatyard in North Carolina. When I was a kid, he used to take me sailing. I loved being on the water."

"I would never have guessed that," Cinnamon said. "You look so comfortable on your television show. I thought you'd have always been interested in reporting."

So, she watched him. "I didn't," he told her. "Not always. There was a time I wanted to be a doctor."

"What happened?"

"I discovered reporting and knew I wanted to search for the truth more than anything else. What about you? I never would have taken you as holding a doctorate in meteorology, either. It just shows you can't tell by looking at a person."

"That's true. The first day you came to the house, I thought you were the delivery man. Then when I saw you, I thought you were either FBI or someone from the military."

"FBI? What gave you that idea?"

She shook her head. "I don't know. It was something about the way you stand, the way you carry yourself. You looked regimented, like you've been trained so well that it's become second nature."

"I'm not sure if there's a compliment in there."

"There's not. A moment after I opened the door, I realized the stance was anger."

He laughed. "I was so stressed that day. Allison had been running me around and everywhere I went someone made a comment about my failed attempt at marriage. The dress was the last straw."

"Mac, I'm so sorry. I know I never should have put the dress on, but it was so beautiful."

An Important Message from the Publisher

Dear Reader,

Because you've chosen to read one of our fine novels, I'd like to say "thank you"! And, as a special way to say thank you, I'm offering to send you two more Kimani Romance novels and two surprise gifts – absolutely FREE! These books will keep it real with true-to-life African American characters that turn up the heat and sizzle with passion.

Please enjoy the free books and gifts with our compliments...

Linda Gill

Publisher, Kimani Press

Peel off Seal and Place Inside...

THE EDITOR'S "THANK YOU" FREE GIFTS INCLUDE:

▶ Two NEW Kimani Romance™ Novels
▶ Two exciting surprise gifts

YES! I have placed my Editor's "thank you" Free Gifts seal in the space provided at right. Please send me 2 FREE books, and my 2 FREE Mystery Gifts. I understand that I am under no obligation to purchase anything further, as explained on the back of this card.

PLACE FREE GIFTS SEAL HERE

▶ DETACH AND MAIL CARD TODAY!

168 XDL ERR5   368 XDL ERSH

FIRST NAME   LAST NAME

ADDRESS

APT.#   CITY

STATE/PROV.   ZIP/POSTAL CODE

Thank You!

"Forget it. It's all over now. Allison is married and everything is fine."

He raised his wineglass and toasted. "To misunderstandings."

"And happy resolutions." She clinked glasses with him and they drank.

Mac felt at ease. Cinnamon was the first woman in a long time that he could be friends with. Even though he told her they didn't like each other, he was quickly finding out she was a very interesting person and he wanted to know her better.

"Cinnamon Scott? I thought that was you." A woman, who could have been in her forties but looked younger, came over. She wore a suit of muted violet and silver that reeked of money. Her hair was perfect, with not a strand out of place. Mac recognized the type immediately.

"Janelle!"

Cinnamon stood and the woman came over. The two hugged like old friends.

"It's so good to see you. Are you back? I never thought you'd make it in a small town in Virginia."

"I'm settling in very nicely, thank you," Cinnamon said. She glanced at Mac. "Janelle, let me introduce you to MacKenzie Grier."

They shook hands.

"Janelle is the owner of a cable station here."

"Yes, and I tried valiantly to get Cinnamon to come on board, but she opted for that weather service job in Virginia. Nice to meet you." She smiled.

"Would you like to join us?"

"Well." She looked over her shoulder. "Maybe for a moment. I'm having dinner with some bankers and they are boring."

Mac snagged a chair from a nearby table and assisted her into it.

"So, Mac, you're an easily recognizable person, especially to anyone who has a television set. How did you meet Cinnamon?"

They both laughed. She looked confused. "We were just talking about that," he answered. Mac went on to explain about the wrong wedding gown.

Janelle laughed. "That's precious," she said. "Too bad you can't use it on your show," she said to Mac.

"I'm a political commentator. And besides, this has already been on cable."

Janelle looked over her shoulder again. "I'd love to hear more," she said, standing. Mac stood, too. "But it looks like the bankers have run out of conversation. Great to see you, Cinnamon. And remember you can always come home." She turned to Mac and offered a hand. "Good meeting you." Then she turned and whispered something to Cinnamon before walking away.

"What did she say?" he asked.

"Nothing important."

"Tell me."

"If she wanted you to hear, she'd have said it out loud."

"Still, I want to know."

Cinnamon stared at him. She wore a slight smile that seemed to grow a little at a time.

"Cinnamon."

"All right, but you're not going to like it," she warned.

He waited.

"She said you reminded her of Wesley Garner."

For a moment he was confused. Then he remembered. "The guy who went to Europe?"

Cinnamon nodded and took a drink of wine. Mac recognized when people were hiding things. Observation was his job. He knew Janelle Bruce had not said that. Raising an eyebrow, he gave Cinnamon a skeptical look.

"That's too many words for what she really said."

"All right," Cinnamon responded. "She said you were nice eye candy." Cinnamon smiled again. "And I have to agree with her."

* * *

The house was brightly lit when Mac drove into the circular driveway. The weather cooperated and the day had been warm. The night was crisp and cool. Mac smiled at Cinnamon as he got out of the car and came around to open her door.

"Beautiful place," he said, looking up at the house and the grounds that extended around it.

"It reminds me of Allison and Paul's," she told Mac. He'd said he no longer owned the house in Virginia.

With his hand on her lower back, he guided her toward the wide steps that led to the front door. Cinnamon felt warmth spread through the thin material of her gown and fought to keep her balance.

"By the way," Mac whispered close to her ear. "Have I told you that you look gorgeous in that dress?"

Cinnamon turned to him. "You are going to be trouble tonight, aren't you?"

"I hope so," Mac said, his meaning clear. He slipped his arm around her waist.

Cinnamon was wearing the purple strapless gown. His reaction when she'd come down the stairs an hour ago had been jaw-dropping silence. Maybe he'd just found his voice. Together they continued toward the house.

The party was in full swing when Mac and Cinnamon arrived.

"Cinnamon." Mary Ellen greeted them at the door. The two women hugged as if they hadn't seen each other in decades.

Mary Ellen Taylor was short and thin, but buxom enough to stop traffic even with only an inch of hair. That alone made her striking, but her perfect African skin, high cheekbones and clear brown eyes, added to the sex appeal she'd been born with.

Penn State University had been Cinnamon's undergraduate and graduate school. She and Mary Ellen Taylor had met in the graduate program, although Mary Ellen was in Criminology while Cinnamon studied Atmospheric Operations. Today Mary Ellen worked as a forensic artist, combining her talent in art and her criminal studies.

"You look great." Mary Ellen pushed her back and studied her from head to toe. Cinnamon turned completely around, modeling the bright purple gown. The full skirt flared out as she twirled.

Cinnamon pushed her arm through Mac's as she introduced him. "Meet MacKenzie Grier."

The two shook hands. Cinnamon saw the sly smile her friend gave her. It said, *we'll talk later.*

"Call me Mac," he said, with a charming smile.

Cinnamon felt the power of it flow like sunshine all the way to her toes.

"Welcome, Mac. Cinnamon didn't tell me she was bringing a television personality." Mary Ellen looked at her friend. "I'm glad you could come. Cinnamon will show you around. Enjoy yourself."

With their arms linked, Cinnamon led him into the ballroom. The rooms in Mary Ellen's home were wider than Cinnamon's. The main living room had been cleared of furniture and a dance floor put down. Everyone called it the ballroom.

"Cinnamon!"

She turned as someone called her name. Several of her friends, who'd been dancing, stopped and came over when they recognized her.

She introduced Mac and answered all the standard questions about leaving Boston and living in Virginia. Mac got her a drink and when he returned, Edward Bailey, one of her former colleagues, stared openly at him.

"I thought I recognized you," he said, snapping his fingers as if he'd just remembered. "You'd think, being in television, too, other personalities would be easier to recognize. Ed Bailey." He introduced himself again and offered his hand. Mac shook it. "You host *Keeping it Honest*."

Cinnamon knew it was a statement Mac had

heard countless times, but he was gracious and nodded.

"It's really good to meet you. I guess we get so involved in our own world that we don't really focus on anything outside it."

"Ed is one of the producers at WBSN," Cinnamon explained. Then to Ed, she said, "You two can talk about it later. This is our song and we're going to dance."

They joined everyone on the dance floor. "Thanks," Mac said, taking her into his arms. "I'm sure you did me a favor."

"I thought you needed rescuing. Ed's a nice guy, but he'll keep you talking all night if you let him."

"I'll heed the warning."

Mac's arms circled her waist and he pulled her tightly against him. They swayed to the music. Cinnamon's head naturally rested on his shoulder, as if it belonged there. She melted into him. She didn't need to act as if she liked him. She *did* like him. In fact, she wanted him. The room was crowded, but Cinnamon felt as if she was alone with Mac.

Mac hummed in her ear. "I should remember this song if it's going to be ours."

Cinnamon leaned back and looked up at him. "You know I only said that because—"

"Doesn't matter why." He stopped her. "You called it."

Cinnamon listened. The bandstand had been set up along the wall. Mary Ellen's parties had a format to them. Since the age group of the attendance list covered several decades, the band played a variety of music. Currently they were in the Cole Porter stage, playing "Love for Sale."

She opened her mouth to protest, but he stopped her. "You'll pay for that," she promised. Mac pulled her back in his arms.

"I certainly hope so," he said, and danced her around the floor until the song ended.

Mac proved an excellent escort. He made friends easily and talked with practically everyone. Mary Ellen found her during a period when Mac was elsewhere.

"So, tell me, where did you find him?" She looked across the room to where Mac was speaking with her parents.

"In my backyard."

"Literally?" Her eyebrows went up.

"Not quite. He was on the porch. Angry and ready to skin me alive."

"Ah, sounds promising." She smiled. "I guess this means he's not the same as he is on television?"

"He wasn't immediately. I was wearing his sister's dress and he thought that was a little over the top." Cinnamon explained about the delivery of the wrong gown.

"You have some nerve."

"Well, it worked out. He didn't eat me."

"Give him time. It looks like he wants to."

Cinnamon stared at Mary Ellen, then looked over at Mac. His back was to her. What had Mary Ellen seen? Mac said he was putting their enmity on hold, but there was nothing between them. Sure, he made her hot, but he didn't know that.

At that moment he turned and smiled at her. Cinnamon felt as if the sun had suddenly invaded her body. Her dress might be bright purple, but she outshined it by millions of watts.

"Mac, I hope you're enjoying yourself," Mary Ellen said as he reached them.

"I am," he answered, slipping his arm around Cinnamon's waist. The action was natural, as if the two of them were already lovers. And it didn't go unnoticed by Cinnamon's friend. "I didn't expect to find anyone here I knew and there are several people I've met before. We're having a good time remembering our mutual pasts." He looked down at Cinnamon. "How about another dance?"

Cinnamon didn't answer. She was unable to

speak. She nodded and turned into his arms, letting him excuse them and guide her away. Cinnamon knew Mary Ellen would be on the phone early the next morning wanting every detail of her and Mac's relationship, but for the time being she only thought of Mac.

They danced without talking. The band had moved on from the Cole Porter era and traveled through time to the nineties. Cinnamon recognized the tune, but her mind wasn't capable of determining the title of the song. She was swaying with the music. Something about her had changed in the last few minutes. Mary Ellen had said he looked at her as if he wanted to eat her. Cinnamon hadn't seen anything like that. Did she want to?

She knew how she felt. But Mac? Mac didn't feel that way about her. He'd told her he wanted to take her to a wedding because there was no chance of her wanting anything more from him. He needed her to play a part. That's what he was doing for her. He was playing a part.

And apparently he was good at it. He'd fooled Mary Ellen.

"I Could Have Danced All Night" floated through Cinnamon's brain. She knew exactly how Eliza Doolittle felt after her dance with Henry Higgins.

Mac was not a dialectician, but he could dance. She twirled around across the sidewalk that led to her mother's house. Mac accommodated her by stepping in and partnering her through the music that played in her head.

"I guess I don't have to ask if you had a good time," he said.

"I had a wonderful time." Elongating the word wonderful, she climbed the stairs to the century-old front door and unlocked it. Inside, she turned on the hall light and went through to the high-ceiling living room. "Would you like something to drink—coffee, nightcap, champagne?"

"I think I've had enough champagne, but coffee sounds good."

Cinnamon took off her wrap and stepped out of her shoes. Barefoot she padded to the kitchen and set up the coffeemaker. Mac followed her in and he was opening and closing cabinets.

"What are you looking for?" she asked.

"Tray, cups and saucers, mugs. I thought I'd help."

Cinnamon forgot that Mac was used to helping Allison. It was natural for him to try and help her. She opened a cabinet over the sink. Inside was an array of china cups. "There's a tray on top of the refrigerator."

He got it and began setting it up. When the

coffee was ready, Cinnamon added the pot to the tray and Mac took it. She led him through the living room to the pink room. When she turned on the light, he stared.

Cinnamon laughed. "I told you my mother liked bright colors."

"Yes, but a totally pink room?" He set the tray on a large, low ottoman that served as a coffee table. Mac didn't immediately sit down.

Cinnamon poured the coffee, but Mac stared at the furnishings. There was a huge mural of the world on one wall. It was the only thing in the room that wasn't a shade of pink. The sofa was a sectional that had been made for the room. The ceiling was high and pictures of pink flowers were arranged in matching frames to accommodate the room height.

"Where did she find a pink piano?"

Cinnamon laughed. "It was specially made for this room, like most of the things in it."

Mac sat down and accepted the cup Cinnamon offered him. "Shouldn't the coffee be pink?"

Cinnamon laughed, then she became serious and quiet. Mac looked at her. She moved to the edge of the sofa and put her cup on the tray.

"What is it?" he asked.

"Thanks," she said.

"For what?"

"For tonight. For escorting me. For meeting my friends and winning them over." She remembered how well he seemed to fit into the party and with people she'd known for years. Leaning over she kissed his cheek. It seemed the natural thing to do.

But what happened next wasn't part of Cinnamon's plan.

Mac's free hand combed through her hair and turned her mouth to his. Cinnamon was balanced on her hand, but it wasn't going to support her much longer, not with her body turning to butter. Mac must have put his cup on the table, for his other arm circled her waist and he pulled her closer to him. His mouth never left hers, except to reposition itself and continue the kiss.

He pulled her across him and laid her down on the long sofa. Cinnamon's arms went around him. His mouth did tantalizing things to her. She welcomed his tongue as it tangled with hers. Cinnamon was in Boston, the town she'd fled with a vow that she was off men, but now she was entwined in Mac Grier's arms and loving it. Her legs draped over his, and Cinnamon found it impossible to keep them still. She rubbed them over Mac's. Mac's hands moved down her body. Fire trailed where he touched her. She tried to suppress the moan of pleasure that welled up in her throat, but the combination of his hands and his mouth were too much.

It had been a long time since a man kissed her. She missed it, missed the rush of emotion, the prickle of nerve endings coming alive and pulsating along her skin, missed the feel of a man's arms holding her. Mac slipped his arms around her again, pressing her against him as his mouth continued its onslaught. She'd begun this as a thank-you kiss, a soft touch to express her appreciation, but she hadn't pushed him away when he deepened the kiss, when he took over and showed her exactly what men and women were made for.

Mac finally lifted his mouth. Cinnamon's heart hammered and she was out of breath.

"You're welcome," Mac whispered.

Chapter 7

Mac opened his eyes and immediately knew where he was and what he'd done. "Damn!" He cursed, as he hooked his legs over the side of the bed and hung his head. He hadn't been thinking straight last night. He couldn't blame it on too much champagne because he'd had only one glass. The rest of the night, tonic water had been his only drink.

It was Cinnamon. The magnetism of her. And that dress. He wanted to peel it off her. Expose her body inch by cinnamon-colored inch and lick every bit of skin he found. When she'd leaned forward and kissed him, he was lost. His hands and body took over. Her mouth was like sweet wine, wet, delicious and tantalizingly inviting. He feasted on it. Kissing her was like nothing he'd ever done before. Everything about her felt good, the shape of her, the feel of her dress and the promise of the soft, smooth skin beneath it. Her face was perfect, he liked the way her hair fell over his hands, the weight of her arms around his neck. Mac stopped, shaking his head as if he could dislodge thoughts of her.

Standing up, he moved to the window and looked out on the Boston street. Red maples lined the walkway. A woman passed by with her dog, leash in one hand, a plastic bag in the other. Cars moved slowly down the street. Everything appeared normal. Everything in its place. Everything except him.

His world had been rocked by a kiss.

And now he had to face her, sit before her at a breakfast table and act as if he was able to keep his mind on simple tasks like chewing and swallowing, breathing in and out.

He was no good at the-morning-after conversation. And he and Cinnamon had had no night before. So why did he feel like this was the morning after a night of wild lovemaking?

Dreams, he told himself. What-ifs. Wishing and hoping. Possibilities. Virtual promises.

Mac turned and headed for the shower. It was going to be a long day.

Mac had a house in Georgetown. He'd gone there directly after seeing Cinnamon home. He lived in Washington, D.C., not Indian Falls. He could live and work in Georgetown. That's what he'd been telling himself for the past two weeks. Yet he spent little time at the house. Other than changing his clothes and showering, most of his time was spent in his office.

He looked at his messy desk, tapped out a few words on his computer keyboard. The phone rang.

"MacKenzie Grier," he said into the phone.

"I thought I'd find you there."

Instantly he recognized his sister's voice. "Allison, great to hear from you." He smiled. It *was* great to hear from her. She'd been back a week and he hadn't talked to her. "Are you two settling in?"

"We're fine," she said. "I was wondering about you. You usually spend more time here than in D.C. Is everything all right?"

"Everything's fine," he lied. "I've been busy getting things in order for future shows. And I thought you and Paul needed some alone time. Who needs a brother-in-law hanging around?"

"I'm sure you wouldn't be an imposition. This is still your home."

"Allison, it's your home. Yours and Paul's." They'd been over this ground before.

"Well, you can still come visit. You'd be surprised to find out all that's going on."

"Like what?" He sat up in his chair, bracing himself for bad news. His heart started to pound. Instinctively he knew it involved Cinnamon.

"We heard about Fletcher Caton offering Cinnamon Scott free invitations to her wedding."

"That was weeks ago."

"Well, a few other people have come forward with more wedding freebies."

"Cinnamon isn't engaged."

"Not yet. But she could be soon."

"What?" Mac nearly shouted. "To who?"

"That's *whom,*" Allison corrected. "And I don't know."

"Allison, are you trying to play Cupid again?"

"No." She sounded as if she'd never interfered in his love life. "Apparently, the local papers heard about Fletcher's offer."

"I know. I was there when it happened."

"Now, the story's been picked up by several other papers and they've begun a contest."

"What kind of contest?" Mac asked.

"It's not a real contest."

His sister was being too slow with information on Cinnamon. Or she was baiting him. Mac's blood pressure had gone up several points just at the mention of Cinnamon's name. Squeezing the phone between his neck and shoulder, he pulled up the Internet on his screen and clicked on one of his favorites. It was for *The Weekly*. The screen painted down in a flash. On the front page was a photo of Cinnamon amid a mountain of letters.

Choose Me, stated the headline. Mac forgot his sister and started reading. *Cinnamon Scott was inundated with mail from would-be grooms this weekend. Letters from as far away as Montreal, Canada, were delivered to the Indian Falls resident with proposals of marriage. "We only see this many letters during the holiday season," said Ray Cobb, the postal carrier who delivered the mail.*

"Mac, are you still there?"

"I don't believe this," he said to himself.

"Believe what?" Allison asked.

"Nothing," he said, coming back to his sister. "How long has this been going on?"

"Since we came back from our honeymoon. It started before we got here."

"What's Cinnamon doing with these letters?"

"You know about the letters?"

"I just read it on the Internet."

"I haven't seen her in a couple of days, but she was reading through them, putting them in categories."

She couldn't be considering this, Mac thought. He knew she wanted to marry. She'd told him that much when they were in Boston. But he was sure she was too intelligent to find a husband through a letter.

"Mac, I didn't call to give you the news of what's going on in town."

"Why did you call?"

"To invite you to dinner. Paul and I are having some people over. It's our first party since we've been married and I'd like my brother to be one of the guests."

"When?"

"This weekend. Saturday. Can you come down?"

"I'll be there Friday afternoon," he said without hesitation.

"Good. See you then."

Mac replaced the phone in its cradle. He stared at the computer screen. Stared at the photo of Cinnamon. He was going to Indian Falls.

Now!

Cinnamon recognized the start and stop hic-cupping of the doorbell. Her heart beat like a hummingbird's. It was Mac punching the bell, getting her attention. Cinnamon forced herself not to run to the door and yank it open. Calmly, she approached it as if he weren't trying to get to a fire. As expected, Mac stood there, a suitcase on the porch floor next to him.

"I need a place to stay," he said.

"What?" It was the last thing Cinnamon expected to hear. "I can't stay with my sister and her husband. I wondered if you'd rent me my old room?"

Cinnamon had said she wouldn't do this. The house was hers. She couldn't have Mac running around freely and destroying her peace of mind.

"Why can't you stay with Allison and Paul?"

"I guess that question means you've never been a newlywed."

"And you have?"

"No, but I know what it's like to be a fifth wheel."

"What about the hotel?" Cinnamon suggested.

"There is no hotel in Indian Falls."

Cinnamon knew they couldn't discuss this standing in the doorway. She stepped back. "Maybe you'd better come in."

Mac lifted the suitcase and crossed the threshold.

"I'm not saying yes," she began as they entered the living room. "We'll need to discuss this." She sat down. Mac took the chair across from her. She was glad he didn't sit next to her. It had been two weeks since she'd seen him and finding him suddenly on her doorstep was like finding the crown jewels. She'd missed him. While they had been in Boston, she'd thought their relationship had changed and that he would come back to Indian Falls. But almost immediately upon returning her to her house, he'd gone away and stayed away.

"Your house is larger than this one. I'm sure you won't be in Allison and Paul's way."

"Maybe not, but they're newly married and need their own space."

Cinnamon needed hers, too.

"There's a hotel in Gateville. It's only ten miles away."

"I called them. They're booked due to the cavern festival."

This part of Virginia was riddled with caves. Every summer tourists came in droves to visit the underground sites. The festival had grown to major proportions over the past twenty years. Cinnamon had gone to it once when she visited her father.

"Besides, I work much better here," Mac said.

"Things are a little crazy right now, Mac."

"So I've read."

Her head came up and she looked at him.

"Have you found someone to replace the TBA?"

"I'm considering it."

"You're not serious?"

"Why not?"

"Because there's…" He stopped. Cinnamon thought he was searching for words. "It's not the way people should meet, or choose a life mate."

"And how should they do that?"

"Face to face," he said. "Don't you want to know whether or not you and this person have any chemistry? Whether you like the same things? Fit well together?"

"Of course. I don't expect to marry someone I can't love. But we're getting off the subject."

"I'll make you a deal," Mac said, as if he were the one with the bargaining chip. Cinnamon let him go on even though she knew who was in control. "I'll borrow the room for the weekend and help you go through the letters."

"First," she said. "It's not the weekend. Today is Tuesday."

"Minor point. I have some writing to do. You won't even know I'm here."

"And second." Cinnamon went on as if he hadn't spoken. "What makes you think I want your opinion? I'm perfectly capable of choosing for myself."

"Maybe," he said.

"What do you mean, *maybe?*"

"I work with people all the time. I get press releases and have to be able to ascertain a person's worth by the few sentences he chooses to put on paper. Reading between the lines is a specialty of mine. I'd be an asset in this endeavor."

"You assume I'm not expert in the same field."

"You know weather, but this is about people. And people are my business. I keep it honest," he said. The pun was not lost on Cinnamon.

"I'm a good cook. I can lift heavy packages, or bags of mail. I'm neat in the bathroom, never leave hair in the sink or the toilet seat up. And I need a room."

She laughed. Mac made her laugh a lot. "I suppose anyone who puts the toilet seat down deserves a room," she said.

"Good," he said.

"There are some rules." Cinnamon stopped his elation.

"Go on."

"We don't share a bathroom or any other rooms. This is strictly a business arrangement. In exchange for your help with the letters, I provide you with a room. No board."

"Agreed," he said.

"This arrangement will remain in effect until the weekend."

"At which time," he finished for her, "I will escort you to the dinner party at my sister and brother-in-law's house."

"And then you'll turn into a pumpkin and—"

"Then we'll see whose name we choose to fill in on that invitation," he interrupted. "After that the rest is up to you."

Cinnamon felt as if he'd just handed her over to a marriage of convenience. She wasn't sure she liked Mac being so involved in her life. But she'd agreed to the deal, and there was no turning back.

Initially, she'd been kidding with Mac, but he was serious and now she had him living in her house and helping her possibly choose the man she would marry.

Cinnamon thought of the wedding gown. She imagined herself in it, floating down the aisle and marrying the faceless man who waited for her. Only he wasn't faceless. He turned in the dream to look at her.

It was Mac.

They'd been at it for four days. Mailbags arrived every day, increasing in number with the days. Mac had been true to his word. He hadn't encroached upon her time unless she asked him, except in the matter of the letters.

The newspaper that had started this letter writing campaign hadn't used her address, but everyone in town knew her and even letters addressed to General Delivery ended up on her dining room table.

"I can't believe there are so many desperate men in the world," Mac commented after several hours of sorting letters.

"I beg your pardon?" Cinnamon said.

He glanced at her, then did a double take. "That came out wrong. I don't mean that you aren't worth it. Clearly you are, but who would have thought so many people would offer to marry someone they'd never met?"

"It's the way of the world. Look at all the Internet dating services. Everyone wants to find the perfect match. And remember in some places arranged marriages are still the norm."

"Not for me," Mac said emphatically.

Cinnamon stopped reading and sorting and looked at him. "Mac, you don't mean that."

"I do," he said. "I had my go at marriage. And I'm done."

"Have you ever thought that she might have done you a favor?"

"Leaving me standing in front of three hundred people and just forgetting to show up? Yeah, I can see the favor in that."

"Wouldn't it be worse if she had shown up and the two of you had made each other miserable for years? Then you'd go through divorce. There might even be children involved. It's your ego that's been bruised."

"Bruised? I think beaten into pulp is a more apt description."

Cinnamon went back to the mail. A photo fell out of an envelope. She picked it up and smiled. "He's gorgeous."

Mac pulled the picture from her hand. "Yeah, too gorgeous. No way he needs to find a bride through the mail."

"You know you can stop insulting me anytime now."

Mac turned and looked at her. "It's not you. You're gorgeous, too."

"Why, thank you."

"And this is no way for you to find a husband. If you're so fired up to get married, I know a score of guys. Let me introduce you to some of them. At least you'll find out more than a letter can tell you."

"Thank you," she snapped. "But I think I'll go with the Longfellow approach a little longer."

"Longfellow approach?"

"Oh, go look it up," she shouted.

Cinnamon got up and went into the kitchen. She wanted to be away from Mac. Anger flushed through her system. Why should he think she needed him to introduce her to men? Why would he even think after the way he'd kissed her in Boston that she would take direction from him?

She had been teasing when she'd told him she'd let him help her. It was an exercise to go through the letters. It was fun in the beginning, but now things were getting out of hand. Mac was trying to find her a husband.

And she was falling in love with him.

"Cinnamon."

Mac called her name and she stiffened. Turning around she looked at him.

"Did I do it again?" he asked.

"It's all right. We're never going to get through all those letters. Every day the postman brings more bags."

She passed him and went back into the dining room, which now looked like it was the post office.

Letters had been sorted into piles. Cinnamon took the pile containing photos and began discarding the ones she wasn't interested in.

"What are you doing?" Mac asked, coming back.

"Sorting."

"Why?"

She stopped on one of a guy that could have been a model. "What do you think of this one?"

"Too good-looking."

She dropped the photo and chose another one. "This guy looks like he's worked as a logger."

Mac shook his head. "Too muscular," he said. "He'd probably crush you in bed."

Cinnamon chose another one. The man was ordinary looking.

"Too young," he said. "He hasn't even learned to shave yet."

Cinnamon dropped the pile on the table. "None of these are going to satisfy you, are they?"

"I'm not trying to stand in your way. I think this is not the way to meet a husband, but I'll give you the benefit of my expertise."

At that moment the doorbell rang. Both of them looked toward the door. Cinnamon wasn't expecting anyone, but it wasn't uncommon for people in Indian Falls to drop by unannounced. Wasn't that how Mac had ended up on her doorstep?

She stood up. Mac put his hand on her shoulder. "I'll get it," he said.

Cinnamon lifted the photos again after Mac left her. She read the letter that accompanied the picture of a young man who could double as posterboy for the all-American male. Cinnamon smiled, but she wasn't really interested in choosing a man from the letters. She thought it would be fun to look through the mail, but she never knew so much of it would come. Or that Mac would find it so irritating.

"You're not going to believe this," he said as he returned to the dining room.

"Believe wha—" Cinnamon began speaking, but when she saw what Mac was holding, she stopped short.

He held three dresses in front of him. Three wedding gowns.

"The driver said they're on approval. You can choose anything in the store for your wedding."

For a moment Cinnamon was stunned. Then she burst out laughing.

"This is not funny," Mac told her.

"It is. Mac, don't you see? This isn't real. It's a publicity stunt to garner attention to the stores."

"Keep thinking that," he told her. "All the way to the altar."

Chapter 8

Allison Grier-Mathis decided to hyphenate her name instead of dropping her former identity and taking on another one. Although Allison's house wasn't that far from hers, Cinnamon and Mac had driven there for dinner. The party had been filled with delicious food and conversation, none of it related to the problems that Cinnamon was having with the overzealous shop owners in town.

As things were winding down, Cinnamon helped clear the table. Allison rolled into the kitchen after her.

"How are things going with my brother?" she

asked without preamble. "I see he's wangled a room out of you."

"Just until tonight. He's going back to D.C. in the morning. And he's lending me his expertise with the letters."

"How is that going?" Allison pulled the dishwasher open and began putting dishes inside.

"I'm not sure. Mac is like a father, never finding anyone good enough. He rejects every candidate. Not that I would select any of them anyway. But it's so much fun seeing him get upset over the process."

"So you're really not interested in any of the men?"

Cinnamon stared at Allison. "As your brother tells me, 'no sane woman would choose a husband this way.'"

"And you're a sane woman?"

"Last time I checked."

"I'm glad to hear that."

"Don't be," Cinnamon warned her. "I'm not after Mac, either. He has a wall around him as thick as a fortress."

"But you could break it down."

"Allison, this is not a strategy to get Mac."

"But it could be."

"No," Cinnamon said. "It can't be. While I

wouldn't choose a man from a letter, I also won't trick a man into falling in love with me."

"I'm not sure you'll have to trick Mac. I haven't seen you two in a few weeks and from what I saw tonight, you're already in love with him."

Cinnamon said nothing. Denial was on the tip of her tongue, but she knew it wasn't true. Since the party in Boston, since their kiss in the pink room, Cinnamon had known. Mac must have sensed something since he'd stayed sequestered in D.C. until Allison called him home for a dinner party.

But he hadn't gone to Allison's. He'd come to her, convinced her to give him a room with a flimsy excuse. She'd allowed it because she wanted him around, because she'd fallen in love with him. But Mac was solidly against long-term relationships.

And for her, marriage was a long-term commitment.

Mac opened the door and helped her out of the car as they arrived back at her house. The sky was clear, the moon a huge silvery disc in a starry sky. Cinnamon recognized the smell in the air. The pressure was low and the air system over them was likely to remain in place for a few more days. This meant the weather would remain calm and warm.

"You and Allison had your heads together a long time tonight," Mac said.

"You know, for a man who probes politicians for a living, you're not very good at asking a straight question."

"All right." He stood up straight and looked her directly in the eye. "What were you two talking about?"

"You," Cinnamon answered.

"And what did she say?"

"She thanked me for letting you stay here."

Cinnamon had reached the porch. She opened the door and went inside. Turning on the light, the wedding gowns were the first things she saw. They hung from the dining room door. Cinnamon told herself she'd deal with them in the morning.

"They are beautiful, don't you think?" she asked Mac.

He looked at the gowns and turned away. "Don't do it," he said.

"Do what?"

"Don't try them on. They're not yours."

"I know," she said. Walking over to them, she touched the train of one. It was covered with flower appliques and crystal pleating. Cinnamon imagined herself dancing in it, sure the hemline would flare out and make a beautiful picture.

She turned around and faced him. "If I were to put them on, I could be sure that no angry brother of the bride would show up and annoy me."

"The best you can do is return them. Tell Fletcher and Amanda and anyone else that this charade has gone on too long."

Cinnamon took down at one of the gowns. She held it up to herself. "What do you think?"

"I think you should stop this."

"Mac, we're going to a wedding next weekend. There is going to be a bride there. You aren't going to turn away from her, are you?"

"Of course not."

"Maybe you need some practice. Why don't I try this one on."

"No!" he shouted.

Cinnamon jumped at the harshness of his reply. "All right, maybe that isn't the best course of action."

"I'm sorry," he apologized. "Why don't we call it a night?"

"Good idea."

He left her then and went upstairs. Cinnamon stared at the dress in her hand and at the papers covering her dining room. She heard Mac moving around upstairs. Moving to the light switch, she turned it off. Immediately the room was plunged into darkness. The only reflection came from the outside lights.

The hem of the dress seemed to jump out at her. Its whiteness contrasted with the other fabric. Impulsively, she pulled the dress she was wearing off and stepped into the wedding gown. Unlike Allison's gown, this one had a zipper and Cinnamon pulled it up her back to the base of her neck.

There was a mirror in the hall, near the front door. Cinnamon went to it. Without turning on the light, she stared at her reflection using only the subdued light from the porch that spilled through the moon window at the top of the door and through the cut glass angles of the beveled glass. She turned around, looking at herself from all angles. Then she waltzed back into the living room, her arms up and around an imaginary partner.

She didn't hear Mac return until he spoke to her. "I knew you couldn't resist."

Stopping suddenly, she turned and faced him. He made a sound, but Cinnamon didn't know if it was surprise or just an intake of air.

"Dance with me?" she asked, taking a step toward him.

Mac moved back. Cinnamon wondered if it was from fear.

"Not a good idea."

"Come on, what can one dance do? You've danced with me before and you'll have to dance with me at the next wedding we go to."

She walked into his arms and they closed around her of their own volition. Mac said nothing about missing music. The two of them began to dance. Again Cinnamon experienced the sensation of being lost in his arms. She wanted to feel it again, wanted to make sure that what she'd felt in his arms in Boston would return if he held her again.

She wasn't disappointed.

Mac's arms moved. He relaxed and slipped them tighter around her. He pulled her securely against him. Her head rested against his chin. They moved together, swaying to the music of her heart. She wasn't sure when things changed, when their feet ceased to move and their heads moved back so they faced each other. She wasn't aware of time passing, of music stopping, of the soft buzz in her ears that blocked out any other sound.

She was aware of her heart, hammering in her chest. She wondered if Mac could hear it. She was aware of her lips, of the tingling sensation that covered them, of the soft warmth that was building inside her. She was aware when Mac's head moved toward her. Aware of the moment when she knew he was going to kiss her. Of the exact moment when she knew if he stopped she'd die.

His hands came up and cupped her face. For an eon he stared into her eyes. She saw the need in his, saw the decisions he made. Cinnamon couldn't move. Anticipation poured into her blood like a narcotic. She wanted him to kiss her as much as she wanted to take the next breath.

His mouth took hers, fast and hard. Hands dug into her hair as he seared his mouth to hers. Whatever was leashed inside him had been freed. His tongue dipped into her mouth, tasting, taking, sweeping aside any protests she might have made. Cinnamon had been here before. She wanted it again. She wanted the raw power of him, the unbridled wrath of his body.

Mac's arms tightened around her, pulling her into full contact with him. She felt the tightness of his muscles, the bulge of his erection through the lace and satin of the wedding gown. Her back arched as torrents of sensation sailed through her. Her blood raged, stormed through her system as something new, something never tested, never seen before took over and drove her upward.

The snap happened in her, too. She felt Mac's hands lowering the zipper on the dress. He moved slowly, contrastingly different from the forces within her, forces that drove her to tear at the fabric, pull it free of her body, so she could connect with the smooth, hardness of his.

Her hands found the bottom of his shirt and rushed under the material to find his skin. The need to touch him, to know his flesh, was overwhelming. Fingers that had turned into nerves, scoured over his back and around his belly. She looped them in his waist band and skimmed them around his body, feeling the tightness in him, hearing the sounds in his throat that added confidence to her actions.

He stopped her fingers, pulling her hands together, then slipping the mutton sleeves of the dress down the length of her arms until it fell to her waist and slipped in silence to the floor. Cinnamon wore only a bra and panties. Mac's eyes moved over her slowly from tip to toe.

Cinnamon's body tingled. She felt her breasts tighten as his mouth kissed her skin, his lips traveling to new points. Mac lifted her and carried her to the steps. Without thinking, Cinnamon let him take her upstairs. Mac went to his bedroom. He carried her across the threshold and let her slide down his body. Cinnamon slipped her hands up his shirt and continued until the fabric was no longer covering him.

She reached for the snap on his pants and pulled them free of any closure. Pushing them down his legs, he stepped free of them for the space of time it took to free himself of the fabric. Then she was back in his arms, as if he couldn't live without the touch of her, without being so close that air didn't pass between them.

Fingers deftly unhooked her bra and Mac's mouth covered her nipple. Sounds issued from her, new sounds, utterances that Cinnamon had not heard before and was surprised to find coming from her throat. It was all Cinnamon could do not to scream. She was ready. She wanted him now!

Through some unspoken communication, Mac understood. Hot hands slipped her panties over her hips, and he lifted her onto the bed. Joining her there, he continued the love-torture, lying with her, running his hands over her nerve-laden body, bringing to life zones of need that she'd never felt before.

Cinnamon didn't see him get the condom. She heard the soft explosion of air as he tore the foil package. Protecting them, he swung his body and joined with hers. A cry of pleasure, uncurbed, unchecked and howling, burst from her at his entry. He began the timeless rhythm, but she quickly reversed their roles. She rode him, rode him hard, holding his shoulders and pumping herself over him as if her life depended on it. And her life did. She had to have him, had to have this man. She understood that. Somewhere in her sex-blurred mind was a sense, a tonic, an elixir that reached out for him, one that let her know, with massive amounts of infusion, that they had the chemistry.

Mac shouted her name. His hands took her waist, his hips pumped upward into her with powerful strokes. Her body took him, took all of him. Time after time the ritual continued, went on and on until Cinnamon thought the two of them could no longer stand the pounding. Yet they went on. Like the forces of a hurricane, their bodies swirled around in strong circles. And then Cinnamon felt it. The roar within her, the rush of rapture like a huge wave building and building until the pressure was so great it had to be released.

The explosion happened in a burst. Mac shouted out and together they collapsed against each other. Their bodies glistened. The room smelled of sweat and sex, a combination so heady it added to the high their joining had produced. Pushing her hair away from her face, she lay in Mac's arms, unable to tell if the thumping she heard was her heart or his.

She closed her eyes, contented, sated, cradled against him and wondered if anyone in the world had ever felt the way she did.

* * *

Cinnamon's eyes popped open at the sound of the doorbell ringing. She sat up in bed, holding the covers to her naked breasts. Mac lay beside her, his eyes wide open, his body as relaxed as if he were scheduled for a massage.

Cinnamon jumped out of bed and ran to her own room. Pulling on jeans and a heavy T-shirt over her bare body, she grabbed a brush and headed for the stairs. Pushing the brush through her hair, she entered the foyer and set it on the small table. She refused to look in the mirror. If her reflection said she'd spent the night making wild love to Mac, she didn't want to know it was visible to the naked eye.

"Good morning, Cinnamon. Glad you're home." Conner Anderson, called Connie by everyone in town, stood on her porch. Cinnamon wasn't fully awake, her eyes were open, but her body was still upstairs, in bed with Mac, warm and ready for him to make love to her again. But Connie didn't know that.

He brushed by her, carrying a black package of stackable boxes. Cinnamon dreaded what she knew was in them.

"Connie, is that what I think it is? Are you crazy to be carrying that stuff around?" She sank into the sofa.

"Calm down, Cinnamon. You're not in Boston anymore." He set the boxes on the coffee table. Taking a chair in front of her, he opened the top one.

Cinnamon gasped when she saw the glittering stones. Connie proceeded to open and set one ring set after another in front of her.

"What are these?"

"They're engagement rings and wedding bands. For your wedding."

Out of the corner of her eye, Cinnamon saw Mac coming from the kitchen. The dining room doors were closed. She hadn't seen him close them, yet she was grateful that their discarded clothes from last night were concealed behind them. Cinnamon wanted to kiss him for his thoughtfulness.

Several minutes later, Mac carried three mugs of coffee, two in one hand, as he entered the room. Cinnamon was fighting to understand what Connie was saying and getting her heart under control. She'd learned tonight that it took her a while to come down from the point Mac carried her to when he made love to her. She wanted his warm body pressed against hers. She wanted Connie to leave so they could have the house to themselves, so they could return to the warm bed upstairs that was holding the remnants of their joining and beckoning them to return for another session of life as it had never been known.

"Morning, Mac," Connie said, setting the tray on one of the unused chairs. "I heard you were down for the week."

"Allison and Paul are back," he said.

Cinnamon clamped her teeth together. She wondered if Connie's comments meant that Mac was here, in Zahara's house, *her* house.

"I've seen them. You can just see how much they love each other."

"True," Mac said. He looked as fresh as if he'd taken a shower and carefully dressed himself, except for his bare feet. He nodded at Connie and passed the cups of coffee to them. Cinnamon gripped her cup as if it were a lifeline. Testing the heat, she sipped the liquid and felt its warmth go down her throat and spread out in her chest.

"Glad you're both here." Connie went back to business, although they had no business. "Cinnamon, we'd like you to choose a setting."

"Connie, you understand I'm not getting married. That I'm not engaged. The newspaper story is a joke."

"Sure, sure," he said. "But you will get married someday and our store is willing to give you and the lucky man…matching rings."

Did he look at Mac when he said that? Cinnamon wasn't sure, but she thought she saw it. Was it an innocent acknowledgment of him being in the room, or was Connie making a subliminal suggestion?

Still Cinnamon couldn't resist looking at the tray when Connie lifted one and set it in front of her.

"They're so beautiful," she whispered as if the occasion called for reverent voices.

"Cinnamon, you're not getting married," Mac said. His voice was stronger than she'd heard it before. It seemed to snap her out of admiring the stones.

She closed the lid on the box she was looking at and faced Connie. "Mac is right. I have no need to choose a setting yet. Maybe when and if I get engaged, I'll choose a wedding ring, but not now."

"You seem to like these." Connie closed one tray, but did nothing about the others that were lying on the table. "Why don't I leave these for you to look at later?"

"Thank you, Connie, but no. Even if this isn't Boston, I'm not going to be responsible for this jewelry."

"And shouldn't the bride *and* groom choose the rings?" Mac asked.

"They do it both ways," Connie said. "Some guys like to surprise their fiancées. They study stone sizes and settings, trying to determine what is best. Other couples choose the rings together. I thought Cinnamon would like to see some of the choices available." He glanced at her. "You don't have to make a decision now. I can leave these for a while."

"They are beautiful, Connie." She took a moment to admire them again. "But I'm not having them here. I wouldn't sleep thinking something could happen to them."

"I understand," he said. "I work around them all the time. But people who don't can get nervous."

Connie was holding an engagement ring with a stone that must be five carats. "Try this on. It only came in a week ago."

Cinnamon gasped again. The size of the diamond was overwhelming. And it wouldn't hurt anything to try it on. She took the ring and looked at it. "I don't think it's the right size."

"That's easily fixed," Connie said in a voice that sounded like he was making a sale.

"Cinnamon."

She heard the warning note in Mac's voice, but ignored it. Looking at him, she saw strange emotions flitter across his features before they settled into an unreadable mask. Her fingers slipped and the ring dropped. It rolled to where Mac stood. He reached down and retrieved it. Two steps brought him to where she sat. He offered her the ring.

Cinnamon didn't know why she did it, but she stuck her finger out. She heard his soft sigh as Mac set his coffee cup on the table in front of her. He slipped the ring on her finger.

"There," Connie said. "Maybe you'll have a groom sooner than you think."

Chapter 9

"Take them off, Cinnamon." Mac stood in front of the fireplace. Connie had just left and Cinnamon returned from the foyer.

"What?"

"The rings. You should have given them back, but since you didn't, take them off and put them away."

"I will not." She stretched her hand out in front of her and admired the glittering setting. "They're beautiful."

"It's getting to you, isn't it?"

"What's getting to me?" She looked at him with skepticism.

"The wedding. The whole idea of the rings, the gown, the flowers. It's getting in your blood."

"Mac, you're just jaded." She gathered the coffee cups and walked past him to the kitchen.

"I'm not jaded."

"Sure you are. I've been expecting this."

"Expecting what?"

"You." She paused. "The closer we get to this wedding, the more uptight you get."

"Uptight? You think what we did last night was uptight?"

Cinnamon slammed a cup on the counter. "I'm not talking about last night and you know it."

"Do you see that you're only helping them along with this…this charade."

"Yeah." She smiled. "But you have to admit, it's a lot of fun." She looked at the rings again. "I have the rings, the dress, the invitations. I'm sure we can make a deal on the flowers and the church. Wanna marry me, Mac?"

"No!" he shouted.

Cinnamon jumped at the force of it. "Okay," she said. "It was a joke, and I forgot that you have no sense of humor."

"I have a sense of humor."

"But not where weddings are concerned?"

He said nothing, only gave her a pointed stare.

"What is it hurting, Mac? A few shop owners get a little publicity and it brings business into their stores. In the long run, it keeps Indian Falls healthy and you apparently love living here."

He seemed to weigh her words before he spoke. "Until something goes wrong."

What could go wrong, Cinnamon asked herself. She turned to the sink and rinsed a cup. Mac came up behind her and circled her waist. He pulled her back against him and slipped his hands under her T-shirt. Immediately, they cupped her breasts. She sank back against him, weightless. Every ounce of resistance left her. Emotions flooded her with the memory of the miracle that had happened last night. Could they do it again? Or were you only allowed one miracle in a lifetime?

Cinnamon's head fell back on his shoulder. Her eyes closed. Arousal flowed over her like a sun bursting into existence. Her hands were butterfly wings as she tried to find the handle to turn off the running water. She found the handle. The sound ceased in her head and she whirled in Mac's arms.

Her mouth found his and she anchored herself to him. Cinnamon had never been forward, but now she couldn't stop herself. Her legs curled around Mac's. She rubbed them up and down his jean-clad limbs. Cinnamon went up on her toes, Mac lifted her off her feet and she circled his body with her legs. His hands cupped her bottom and caressed her. He pressed her against the sink while his mouth continued to devour hers. Cinnamon found the magic of the night before. It came to her the same and yet differently. A new day, new sensations, a new boldness to their discovery of each other.

Mac sat her on the edge of the sink and moved back only far enough to pull the T-shirt over her head. He threw it behind him. Cinnamon didn't see it fall to the floor. Mac lifted her again and took her upstairs, where she discovered a second miracle.

"What could go wrong?" Cinnamon had been confident when she'd asked herself that question. Now she wasn't so sure. Usually as soon as those words were said, something was bound to backfire. In Cinnamon's case, it took a week before it happened. Mac didn't return to Washington at the end of the weekend. And he didn't move out. Cinnamon could have made a point of it, but she didn't. She thought of broaching the subject of their living arrangement, but quickly let the thought go.

She liked knowing Mac was there, even though they hadn't been to bed together since that night and the following morning. That magical, crazy, wild time when he'd rocked her world. Thoughts of them together stole into her mind at odd moments. She'd find herself looking for him to join her for a meal or sit out on the porch. When he wasn't around, she'd fantasize about him.

She'd been fantasizing several moments ago, when he'd walked into the living room, dressed in a dark suit and with an even darker expression. It was wedding day, the culmination of a week of him dreading all things nuptial. Cinnamon had been dressed for an hour, and she'd called to Mac several times letting him know they were going to be late. She thought he was intentionally avoiding going, but he was in the wedding party.

"Do you have a gift?" she asked. Until this morning, she hadn't thought of a wedding present for the couple. Cinnamon didn't know them. They were Mac's friends. And consequently, he should be the one thinking of a gift. With him in the house, her thoughts constantly flew to him, surrounded his habits, discovered the little things he did and didn't do.

"No," he finally said. "I'll just write them a check. Isn't that what people do these days?"

"It's easier," she said, her tone flat. "You'll

need a card. Maybe we can stop at Fletcher's and pick up one."

That was the way the day had begun and it didn't get any better after they got to the ceremony.

Weddings were great social occasions. Cinnamon didn't know how much time it had taken to plan the perfect day, but the ceremony was held in a grand church near Rock Creek Park in the center of D.C. A small intimate setting for three to four hundred of the bride and groom's closest friends. Mac had left her and gone with the rest of the wedding party. As guests arrived and were escorted to seats, Cinnamon noticed Mac never performed this duty.

She wondered where he was. His hands had been ice cold when he'd left her. She checked her watch and noticed the time for the wedding to begin had come and gone. Cinnamon pursed her lips, wondering if everything was going all right with the wedding party. She sat in the middle of the packed church. Turning around, she tried to see the back of the building, tried to get a glimpse of the groomsmen. Did anyone look more nervous than usual for a day like this? She saw nothing.

Her eyes moved over the guests. Somewhere in the congregation was Mac's former fiancée. Cinnamon wondered which one she was. She'd

seen no signs of her, other than Mac's attitude.
No photos of them together enjoying some moment he wanted to preserve had been at Allison's
or in the room he used at her grandmother's.
Cinnamon scanned faces and the backs of heads,
wondering about the woman who'd captured
Mac's heart.

And ruined him for any other woman.

Time continued to move. Half an hour went by
and people were shifting in their seats. Conversations rose over the organ music as the fear that
something was wrong became tangible.

Fifteen minutes later, Mac appeared in the door
escorting a slightly overweight woman wearing a
pale-yellow chiffon dress that floated about her as
she moved. Her face held a broad smile, but her
features looked strained. She took a seat in the front
row. She had to be the mother of the bride. Cinnamon
took a breath. This meant the entire wedding party
was here and the ceremony would begin.

Mac didn't come back up the aisle, but went
toward a back door that led behind the altar.
Cinnamon looked at his face as he moved. He
stared directly in front of him, looking neither left
nor right. Cinnamon peered at the guests, wondering which of them was more interested in Mac
than the others. A wave of jealousy snaked through

Cinnamon as she spotted a woman several rows in front of her. She must be Jerrilyn McGowan.

The ex-fiancée.

Finally the groom and best man came out from the vestibule. Cinnamon breathed easier. Everything was going to be fine. The music rose and the procession started. Cinnamon gave her attention back to the ritual, yet watched closely as Mac took his place and looked out over the congregation.

It was a storybook ceremony. After the late start, everything was a well-directed play. Cinnamon kept her eyes on Mac. The other members of the wedding party stood straight, but relaxed. In contrast, Mac was rigid.

Cinnamon listened to the vows as if they were being spoken to her, all the while her eyes were trained on Mac's back. Once he looked over his shoulder. She couldn't tell if he was trying to connect with her, as she wished, or if he sought someone else in the church.

The bride and groom kissed and started up the aisle as husband and wife. The guests filed out, meandering around in small groups that eventually headed for the reception hall while the traditional photographs were being taken. Cinnamon waited near the car.

Finally the wedding party appeared, piling into

waiting limousines. She stood up straight as Mac headed toward her. She didn't know how to read him. Was he still upset about being here? He opened her door and helped her inside without a word. As he got in and pulled out of the parking lot, Cinnamon wouldn't have been surprised if he turned the car toward home and skipped the reception altogether.

But he didn't.

"The bride was late," he finally said, answering her unasked question. Cinnamon wondered what the forty-five-minute delay was for. Traffic in the District was always a problem, but she didn't think it was that.

"You didn't think she was coming?"

"The thought occurred to me. That was why I was at the back of the church. It took so long that Richard asked me to go and see what the holdup was. The bride arrived as I got there."

"Was that why you escorted her mother to her seat?"

He nodded. "I needed to get back to Richard as soon as possible. Going through the church was the quickest route."

"I'm glad it turned out all right," she said.

"So far."

"Mac, you can relax now. The ceremony is over.

From here on, it's a party. Everyone will be thinking of the bride and groom. No one will be talking about you."

"Maybe," he said. "Maybe not. Jerrilyn was in the audience. I saw her when I took Mrs. Tate to her seat."

"But you were expecting that," Cinnamon reminded him.

He nodded so slightly that she could have thought he forgot. Cinnamon wondered whether he was truly over her. They'd made love and she was sure Mac hadn't used her as a substitute, but he'd been engaged to Jerrilyn, and wanted to marry her. The emotions within him had to be strong. Maybe they were still as strong as they had been two years ago. Maybe he really wanted to marry her despite the way Cinnamon had felt in his arms.

They pulled into the parking lot of the reception hall directly behind the other cars in the wedding party. Mac helped her out. He had duties and for a time Cinnamon was separated from him. The reception was inside a ballroom that was designed for large groups. The garden had been decorated with flowers and ribbons and more photos were taken out there.

Cinnamon knew no one at the reception. She

wandered about alone for a while, then joined the end of the reception line.

"Congratulations," she said when she reached the happy couple. Both looked as fresh and happy as if she were the first person in the reception line. "I'm with MacKenzie Grier."

"He told us about you," the bride said, shaking her hand. Cinnamon moved farther down the line, wondering what Mac had said.

The line broke up as she got to the last member of the party. Mac was instantly by her side.

"How are you doing?" she whispered.

"Fine, now that everything is over."

The traditional bride and groom dance came next. Everyone watched for half the song, then the floor was flooded with people.

"Dance with me?" she asked.

Mac took her in his arms and squired her around the floor. He said he was fine, but she felt the tension in his arms as they held her.

"Look at me," she told him. His eyes looked into hers. "Relax. Just look at me and move your feet."

After a while, she felt the tautness leave him. His arms closed around her waist and they swayed to the music. He continued to look at her, blocking out everything else. Cinnamon thought she was getting the Mac she knew back. But as the music ended he pulled her arm through his and turned to lead her off the floor. Suddenly the arm she was holding tensed. Cinnamon looked at him and then followed his gaze. A woman, dressed in a royal-blue suit, walked toward them. She wasn't the one Cinnamon had seen in the sanctuary and thought was Jerrilyn McGowan. That woman was pretty. This woman was beyond gorgeous. She moved with confidence, her smile double wattage.

"Mac, it's great to see you." She didn't extend her arm to shake hands or move to hug him as friends often did when they hadn't seen each other in a long while.

"Jerrilyn," he said with a slight nod.

Something akin to pain went through Cinnamon. This was Jerrilyn. This was the woman Mac had been in love with, might still be in love with.

"Jerrilyn McGowan," she said, looking at Cinnamon. This time she did extend a hand.

"Cinnamon Scott." Cinnamon accepted her hand. She had to lean forward since Mac had her left arm pressed into his side.

"I suppose Mac has told you our story?" she asked.

"Yes," Cinnamon said.

Turning her attention to Mac, she said, "We were

just as happy as Richard and Sandra," she said. "We should have gone through with the wedding."

"It wouldn't have worked, Jerrilyn," Mac told her.

"It could have," she said.

Before Mac could reply, a man came up carrying two glasses of wine. He gave one to Jerrilyn.

"You remember Perry Laurance?" Jerrilyn said.

"Hello, Mac." Perry greeted them with a smile. "Good to see you again." The two men shook hands.

"This is Mac's date," Jerrilyn said. "I'm sorry, I've forgotten your name."

"Cinnamon," she supplied. "Cinnamon Scott."

"I can see she's more than Mac's date," Perry said. Cinnamon tightened her hand on the arm Mac was holding.

"Congratulations, Mac." He indicated the ring on Cinnamon's finger. "Wow, that's the largest diamond I've ever seen."

Cinnamon held her breath. She waited for Mac to deny an engagement, waited for him to tell them the truth, but Mac said nothing.

"It's beautiful," Jerrilyn said, staring at Cinnamon's hand. She looked a little taken by surprise. Cinnamon wondered if she was jealous that her ring hadn't been this large.

The diamond was real and it was disgustingly large, but it wasn't a real engagement ring. Cinnamon loved the feel of it on her finger. There were times she pretended she really was engaged to Mac. She hadn't thought that maybe he had the same fantasy. And moments ago it had become real.

"Well, it was good seeing you again, Mac," Jerrilyn said. "And congratulations on your wedding. I wish you well."

She and Perry turned and strolled away. Cinnamon felt the air go out of Mac's body. It was over.

"First time?" she asked.

He nodded. "I thought it would be worse."

"She's beautiful, Mac." Cinnamon could see how he'd pursue her. The two would make a beautiful couple.

"Not inside," Mac said. "Not in her heart, where it counts."

Without asking, Mac turned Cinnamon back into his arms for another dance. Cinnamon wanted to ask about the impression he'd left with his former fiancée. The two were not engaged, yet he'd let Jerrilyn leave believing they were.

As the dance ended, Cinnamon called his name. He looked at her, but quickly turned away as someone else called to him.

"Mac!" The newly married Briscoes rushed over to them. "Why didn't you tell us?"

Sandra and Richard Briscoe nearly glowed with pleasure. "Let me see the ring," Sandra commanded.

She grabbed Cinnamon's hand and pulled it into view. Richard stared at the size of the stone and looked at Mac.

"What is that, a mortgage?" he asked. They all laughed. The former Sandra Tate, now Sandra Briscoe, pulled Cinnamon into her arms as if they had been friends for years.

Cinnamon was no longer finding this funny. A pretend engagement was one thing. They'd agreed to go as friends. And nothing more. But now…what was this? And more people knew; believed.

"I am so happy for you." Sandra hugged her again. Richard pumped Mac's hand. "You should have told us. I guess this means all that stuff with Jerrilyn is behind you."

Sandra elbowed her husband.

"Sorry," he said.

"It's all right," Mac told him.

"What's going on here?" Several people who had seen Richard and Sandra's actions drifted over.

"Mac's getting married," Richard explained.

"Mac, you're engaged?" someone asked.

More people glanced over shoulders and pushed forward to see the ring on Cinnamon's finger. He'd been asked the point-blank question.

Cinnamon waited to hear his answer with as much anticipation as his friends.

"Finally, going to take the plunge again?" one of the groomsmen asked, accompanying his statement with several slaps on Mac's back.

"You can't run away forever," Mac said. He introduced her to the crowd. "This is Cinnamon Scott, my fiancée."

Cinnamon accepted the smiles and hugs, people shaking her hand and strangers kissing her on the cheek. She could barely hold in the tension coiled in her stomach. How was Mac going to get them out of something like a fake engagement?

News of their engagement spread through the crowd faster than a gale force wind. Cinnamon discovered these people thought highly of Mac. She was repeatedly invited to dance. And every man who took her to the floor gave her the same congratulatory speech. They told her how great a man Mac was and how Jerrilyn had abandoned him at the altar.

She was sure she gave the right responses, but she didn't remember them. She was thinking about Mac, checking to see where he was. They needed to talk.

This was her fault. She shouldn't have worn the ring. Without it, the circumstances they were in now would not have occurred. But Cinnamon had been too afraid to leave it behind. Looking at it, she twisted it on her finger. It gleamed in the light.

And it connected her to Mac.

As the bridal party took their seats for the formal meal, Cinnamon found her place card at her assigned table and took a seat. She looked around to see if anyone was noticing Mac, whispering about him and Jerrilyn, looking to see if they were together or getting together. All eyes seemed to be on the bride and groom. All except one person's. Jerrilyn sat at a nearby table. Her gaze was directed at Mac despite the man leaning next to her and whispering in her ear.

A rush of jealousy went through Cinnamon. Her eyes went to Mac. He sat on the dais, but he wasn't returning Jerrilyn's stare. Cinnamon forced herself to take a breath. She wished she could go to him, put her arms around him and let him know that he had her support. As if he heard her wishes, his eyes met hers. She smiled and he returned it with a quick grin. It told her that he wished this was over and that he had never agreed to stand up for his friend. But it was too late for that.

"Hello." A woman came and sat next to

Cinnamon. "I'm Roxanne Goodman. I'm with Case. He's in the wedding party."

"Cinnamon Scott. I'm with Mac. He's also in the wedding party."

"I know. I saw you two when you arrived before the wedding. Case and I got here at the same time."

"Hi, Roxanne," another woman said as she found her name and took a seat across from them.

"Gloria," Roxanne acknowledged. "It's become a tradition to seat the dates, wives and husbands of the wedding party at the same table," Roxanne explained. "Gloria is engaged to James."

Cinnamon nodded and looked at the head table. She didn't know Case from James or any of the groomsmen except Mac.

"James is sitting next to Mac," Gloria supplied, pointing him out.

Cinnamon looked at the man next to Mac. He was as tall as Mac, but had a huge smile on his face. He looked like a practical joker. Gloria gave him a small wave and he nodded. Mac's expression was unreadable.

Turning back to the table, Gloria asked. "Have you met Jerrilyn yet?"

"Gloria!" Roxanne chastised.

"It's all right," Cinnamon said. "I've met Jerrilyn. She's beautiful."

"Yeah, but Mac never gave her a ring the size of the one you're wearing," Roxanne said, apparently having gotten over her decision that talking about Jerrilyn was in bad taste. "I'll bet she's green with envy."

"It's her own fault," Gloria said. "Mac was at the wedding. She was the one who chose not to show up."

Cinnamon wanted to listen. She wanted to hear every detail of Mac's life, but she decided it wasn't fair. "Do you mind if we don't talk about that?" she asked.

Gloria shrugged. "Sure," she said.

"I'm sorry," Roxanne said. "Gloria didn't mean to upset you. So, how long have you and Mac been engaged?"

No matter where she turned at this reception, Cinnamon thought, someone was asking about her engagement to Mac. She'd barely had time to get used to the new rules that went along with being engaged. Thankfully, Mac wasn't sitting next to her, but eventually the two would be together.

"Not long," Cinnamon answered truthfully. She kept her face straight when she said it, but looked at the ring to camouflage the lie of omission that might be visible on her face. The truth was their engagement was not even an hour old.

And it wasn't real.

Most of the traditional rituals had been done when Mac left the dais. Only the bride's bouquet and garter remained to be thrown. And, of course, the cutting and eating of the bridal cake would be the last act. For those, Mac didn't need to sit in front of the guests looking like a target for everyone to shoot at.

He'd divided his time between watching the audience and watching Cinnamon. She kept twisting the ring on her finger. While Mac hadn't given it to her, he was sure her action was due to him telling Jerrilyn they were engaged. He couldn't explain why he'd done it. The words were out of his mouth before he could stop them. He knew it was lashing out at Jerrilyn, but that was only part of it. He wanted people to think he was over her. That her actions at their wedding hadn't affected him.

In the process he'd used Cinnamon.

And he was kidding himself and everyone else. How could anyone not be changed by such an experience?

Mac headed for Cinnamon. She stood several

feet from him talking to a group of his friends. He liked it that she seemed to fit in to the scene, that she felt comfortable taking care of herself while he performed his groomsman duties. She was totally unlike Jerrilyn, who had to be attached to him from the moment they arrived until they left. He excused himself to pass a couple en route and found Jerrilyn stepping into his path.

"How about a dance?" Jerrilyn asked.

Cinnamon chose that moment to look for Mac. Their eyes met and he saw the smile on her face freeze as Jerrilyn put her arms around his neck. Cinnamon gave him an *I understand* smile and went back to her conversation.

Mac pulled Jerrilyn's arms from his neck. The fact that several people's eyes were on them wasn't lost on him. Taking her hand, he danced with her.

"Is this another game, Jerrilyn?"

"Why, Mac, you can't still be angry." Pushing herself back, she stared up at him. "It's been two years."

"Why, Jerrilyn?" Mac asked the question he'd been waiting two years to have answered. "Why did you wait until everyone was at the church? If you didn't want to marry me, you had ample opportunity to call it off."

"I had every intention of coming. I had the dress

on. My hair was done. My father was there. Everyone was ready. But I just couldn't. I wasn't sure. Don't you understand, Mac? I had to be sure."

"Jerrilyn, no one is ever sure. Not truly."

"I am now."

Light dawned in Mac's brain. His feet stopped moving. Jerrilyn stopped, too. They stared at each other.

"Mac, isn't it obvious I'm still in love with you? What I did two years ago was a mistake. I've wanted to tell you that, but I never had the courage until now."

"I'm engaged," Mac said, finding his voice and falling back on the lie he'd told earlier. And one he had not cleared with Cinnamon.

"But you're not married."

Jerrilyn's arms started moving over his shoulders and around his neck. She pressed her body into his. Mac remembered her clinging to him, the way she would wrap herself around him and he thought the world would never be the same.

"What about Perry?" He paused as her arms began a familiar journey. "Doesn't this look a little awkward?"

"Perry and I are past tense. We're only here because we're between relationships."

"Frankly, I'm surprised you found someone to replace me," Jerrilyn said.

"Cinnamon isn't replacing you." Mac glanced across the room at where Cinnamon stood. She was talking to Mr. and Mrs. Tate, but her eyes took in the two of them. "You no longer have a place that needs replacing, Jerrilyn." With that Mac kissed her on the cheek and walked toward Cinnamon.

"Mac, we need to talk," Cinnamon said the moment they got in the car.

"I apologize," Mac told her. "It got out of hand. I never expected Jerrilyn to rush off and tell anyone."

Mac pulled the car into weekend traffic. It was heavy in the District as always. This was the in-between hour. That's what Samara called it. That time period between afternoon events ending and evening programs beginning. People heading for dinner before attending one of the District theaters, or going farther into Virginia or Maryland for one of the theaters there, were pouring onto the roads. Rock Creek Park had an amphitheater where summer concerts took place and there was always something going on to draw tourists onto the many spokes of the giant District wheel.

"What did you expect her to do?" Cinnamon

asked. "Be upset? Crawl into a hole because her former fiancé has moved on?"

"I expected her to say hello, tell me she was sorry and go on her merry way."

"I can't believe you," she said. "Men are such brainless creatures."

"That's not true."

"If it isn't, then why am I here? If you wanted her back, you'd have come alone. And you wouldn't have waited two years to see her again."

"I don't want her back. She offered."

"She did?" Cinnamon was clearly surprised. "She made a play for you? After you introduced me as your fiancée?"

He nodded.

"I'm wearing a ring the size of the Grand Canyon and still she wants you back?" Cinnamon glanced at him. "What did you tell her?"

Holding her breath, she waited for him to answer.

"I told her she'd been replaced."

Cinnamon was stunned into silence. She knew Mac had asked her to come to this wedding because Jerrilyn would be here. Naively, Cinnamon thought it was so he appeared to be involved or becoming involved with someone. She was his protection. He was using her as a buffer between himself and Jerrilyn McGowan.

"Mac, are you still in love with her?"

Mac stopped the car at a traffic light. He turned in his seat and looked at Cinnamon. Darkness was falling. She could see the shadows crossing his face.

"To tell you the truth, Cinnamon, I'm not sure." He raised his hand from the steering wheel and flailed it in the air. "I know it's been two years, but seeing her again today brought back a lot of memories."

That wasn't the answer Cinnamon was looking for.

"Allison says she's wrong for me. She's right. I know that, but it doesn't change how I feel." He paused. "There is one thing I know."

Cinnamon waited for him to continue.

"She's part of the past. I'm not going back there."

A car horn sounded behind them. Mac grabbed the steering wheel and started the car moving again. For a long while he drove in silence. Cinnamon wondered what he was thinking. Was he still in love with Jerrilyn and fighting it? She looked at her hand. The huge diamond stared at her.

Mac reached over and covered her hand with his. It was warm and reassuring.

"Did you get anything to eat?" Mac suddenly asked.

"Not after the announcement."

"Announcement? What announcement?"

She raised her hand. "Our engagement." Cinnamon smiled. "How quickly you forget." She hoped to lighten the mood. "It seemed I danced and talked to everyone, but had no chance to eat."

"Wanna get something?"

"Is there a quiet place where we can talk?"

"Not here," he said.

Cinnamon had forgotten. Mac was a public figure in this town. Any restaurant they went to was bound to have people who knew him or people who recognized him. They could go to Samara's, but Cinnamon didn't like to drop in on her sister unannounced. It was unlikely that Samara would have a man there, but there was always the chance.

"Do you mind Chinese take-out?"

"It sounds wonderful."

"Then I know a place."

Half an hour later they were getting out of the car in front of a house in Georgetown. Cinnamon held the heavy brown bag away from her dress, as grease was inching up the side. Inside Mac turned on the lights and pointed her toward the kitchen.

"This is lovely," she told him, coming back into the living room. "How can you say you only work here? This house has so much character." She looked at the crown molding, the ageless architectural details that defined the space. And the furnishings were comfortable and inviting. Two sofas faced each other in front of a fireplace. Cinnamon took a seat on one of them.

Mac pulled his jacket and tie off and dropped them over a chair. On the mantelpiece was a large photo of Allison.

"I'll get the food," Mac said. "Want something to cover your dress?"

"Have you got a shirt or something I could put over it?"

"I'll see what I can find."

He brought her a T-shirt. Cinnamon took it and went in the bathroom. She removed her dress and pulled the t-shirt over her head. It came to her knees. Finger combing her hair, she left the dress hanging over the shower rod and went back to eat.

Mac didn't say anything when she came back. He was spooning food onto two plates, but she heard the gasp that came from him as he stopped, the spoon in midair.

"I wasn't expecting that," he said.

She sat down and pulled a plate close to her. "Maybe we should talk about this other unexpected turn of events." Cinnamon sat and put a forkful of food in her mouth. She'd never learned to use chopsticks and apparently neither had Mac for they both had forks.

"What are we going to do about this pretend engagement? It'll be all over your office before the night is over."

"I'll endure it," he said.

Cinnamon stopped eating and stared at him. "Endure it?"

"I mean the comments that people make. In a couple of weeks, I'll tell them we called it off."

"You know what they'll think when that happens. That you're a two-time loser. That you can't hold on to a fiancée. That women desert you."

"It doesn't matter," he said.

"Doesn't it? You were so uptight about people knowing you'd been jilted. What do you think this will do for your reputation in this town? Your show is *Keeping it Honest*. How honest have you been?"

Again he appeared to weigh her words. "Well, we can't stay engaged," he said. "And getting married would take it way over the top."

"Yes," she agreed. "We said we'd attend Richard and Sandra's wedding. That we would just be friends until it was over, that there would be no strings. I don't think this is a string, Mac," Cinnamon said. "This is a whole ball of yarn."

"We also said we didn't even like each other. That's not true anymore, either." Mac eyes were tender when Cinnamon looked at him. Her throat closed off. She couldn't eat another mouthful. "You like me now?"

He stared at her for a long moment. "Why don't we stay here tonight. I'll take you home in the morning."

Chapter 10

Whoever thought a day didn't change much had never lived in Indian Falls. Mac found a newspaper on the front step and picked it up as they were going into the house. Opening it, he saw the headline and nearly stumbled across the threshold.

Mystery Man Soon To Be Revealed. Below it was a sketch of a man. Mac wanted to crush the paper. He and Cinnamon had spent a wonderful night together. In fact, since he'd met her all his days had been different, instilled with a kind of magic that had him wanting to see her every day, wanting to be with her all the time.

After eating, they'd gone to the living room and left the lights off. They'd talked. Mac had talked to her like he'd never talked to another woman. After a while she'd asked him a critical question.

"Mac, are you still in love with her?"

Mac didn't answer for a moment. He wanted to weigh his body's reaction—if that rush of emotion he had for Jerrilyn in the past was still there. It wasn't. She'd told him that missing their wedding was a mistake, that she was sure now that she loved him.

But for Mac nothing happened. Slowly he swung his head from side to side. "No," he said, aloud. "I'm not in love with her."

"Are you sure?" Cinnamon asked.

"Very sure," he said. "I'm not sure now that I ever was truly in love with her. I know that our marriage would have failed in the long run. And my feelings for her are not those of a man in love."

Cinnamon had said nothing after he's spoken. The two of them had watched the play of light on the windows from the trees outside and the occasional car that drove down the quiet street. Eventually, she'd fallen asleep in his arms. And he'd carried her to bed.

In the morning she'd awakened beside him. Discovering her next to him had broken a barrier. He

seemed to come alive with her. They'd made love. More than that, he thought. They had discovered a new kind of lovemaking, one that changed his perception of what two people could be to each other.

And now, seeing the newspaper, he discovers that there is someone else. She hadn't mentioned anyone. Yesterday, when they were at his townhouse, it had been perfect, yet she said nothing. Only that they couldn't get married. Was this the reason? Was there another man?

Cinnamon had gone upstairs to change into her own clothes. She came down the stairs wearing khaki pants and a hot pink shirt.

"Who is this?" he asked, thrusting the paper at her.

Cinnamon swallowed hard. "Maybe we'd better talk," she said.

"You're damn right we'd better talk." Mac considered their time together idyllic. He didn't spend time like this with women. At work, he was all business. With other women it was sexual. They went out, made plans to attend things, met for lunch or dinner and had sex. Never had anyone just sat and talked to him, listened to his plans for the future, his goals, dreams and asked him questions about his family because she was interested in him and not interviewing him for a magazine story.

That's the night he'd spent with Cinnamon. They'd fallen asleep in each other's arms and woke up to make love. Or create a new universe, Mac was unsure which one. With her it was different. She completed him.

And now there was a sketch of a man on the front page of *The Weekly*—her fiancé.

He followed her into the dining room, a place filled with the debris of this joke. She sat in front of a laptop computer and opened it up. Her e-mail program came on.

"I didn't tell you because you don't approve of this method. Lately, people have been sending me e-mail proposals. Some of them come with photos. I think someone may have sent a few to the newspaper."

She opened a few messages and showed him the photos popping up.

"Umm, yummy," she said over one of them.

Mac snapped, "Yummy! That's how you describe a man?"

"Well, look at him." She turned the screen toward him. The full color photo filled the screen. The man had long black hair that was layered and gave his face a softened look, high cheekbones, and dimples. "Look at those dimples. They're irresistible. He's yummy. What word would you use?"

"Gay."

Cinnamon laughed. Mac scowled. "He's no more gay than you are."

"How can you tell?"

"I'll show you." Cinnamon reached for the computer mouse. On the graphic image she removed the layer containing hair. The black shoulder-length wavy mass was replaced by a close-cut neat arrangement.

"What are you doing?" Mac asked.

"Just watch."

Layer by layer she removed features from the photo; the high cheekbones became less defined and a wide smile replaced the more serene look. The dimples remained. Hazel-colored eyes converted to chocolate-brown, and the thin mustache morphed into a clean-shaven face. Removing the last layer, added back the lines of character to a face that had seen a few of the world's crises.

Mac's mouth dropped open as the photograph revealed the true man behind the mask—himself.

"Where did you get that picture?"

Cinnamon smiled teasingly. "I have my sources."

"My sister," he answered his own question. "I never sent this letter."

"Of course, you didn't," she said. "It's a joke, Mac. You find something wrong with every man

who's sent a letter. I wondered if you were looking for a Mac clone."

"You think I want to marry you?"

She looked at the photo and then at him. "Not exactly," she said. "I think you want to find someone who's just like you. And since that's an impossibility…"

"You couldn't be further from the truth," he said after a stunned moment. "I'm never going to get married."

"Well, who asked you?"

She got up and went to the door. Turning back she looked at him. "Mac, this arrangement is not working. I'm sorry you don't want to stay at your sister's, but I think it would be better if you left. Today."

Mac didn't see her go up the stairs, but he knew that's where she'd gone. He felt like a heel, like he needed to kick himself. But he'd said nothing wrong. He wasn't getting married.

Ever.

But women wanted to be married. Cinnamon wanted to marry. She'd told him as much when they first met. But he didn't. He'd had his turn at the altar. It was someone else's turn. His friends were making the journey and so far none of them had had the same experience he had. He never

wanted to go through that again. And he never would. No matter how much he—

He stopped. What was he thinking? What was his mind going to tell him. He wasn't in love with Cinnamon. Was that the word he was going to use? No matter how much in love with her he was?

This was a fine mess, he thought.

Cinnamon heard Mac's car door slam shut. The engine roared to life and he reversed down the driveway. He was gone. Going to the window, she looked out. His taillights glowed red as he stopped at the corner and then turned toward the highway. He was going back to Washington, to his house in Georgetown.

She was alone.

She hadn't known how to respond when he'd seen the photo of himself staring from the computer screen. She'd meant it as a joke, thinking Mac would laugh at seeing himself uncovered, layer by layer. She didn't know how the conversation got out of hand. When Mac asked her if she wanted to marry him, she should have shrugged it off, thought of something clever to say, but nothing had come. Unfortunately, she'd told him the truth.

But she hadn't given the enhanced photo to the newspapers. She could probably thank Allison for

that. Allison had done all the masking of the photo and showed Cinnamon how to remove the layers. She was playing Cupid for her brother, and their little joke had backfired.

Big time.

Leaving her room, she walked toward the stairs, but only paused at them before continuing to the last room on the hall.

Mac's room.

She opened the door. Everything was gone. The bed was made, the spread so precisely smooth it looked as if no one had ever slept there, no one had made love there. His computer was gone. The papers that had been spread out on the desk had been removed. The surface was polished and shiny.

The room was empty of everything physical, but Mac was still there. His presence lurked in every corner of the place. She looked over the room, hearing echoes, snatches of conversations they'd had while they pillow-talked after the best sex she'd ever had.

Tears crowded in Cinnamon's eyes. She blinked them away. She'd done the right thing. Even though she felt as if her heart had been surgically removed. She'd done the right thing.

Stepping back, Cinnamon pulled the door closed.

And wept.

* * *

The kitchen cabinets gleamed. The counters and floor shone brightly and were clean enough to eat off of. Every room in the house had been dusted and cleaned to the point of sanitization. For the past week, Cinnamon had done little else. Both inside and outside had received her attention.

She had another month before she officially started work. But she didn't have enough to do to fill the days or the nights until she started. She was going crazy. Even the contest joke didn't amuse her anymore.

Cinnamon put the cleanser and brushes away. It was barely ten o'clock in the morning. They were still serving breakfast at Velma's. She hadn't been there in a while and she could use a good meal. Not that she was hungry, but it was a place to meet and talk to other people.

Showering and dressing quickly, Cinnamon donned a white short set, a blouse with an eyelet ruffle along the hem and shorts that also carried the eyelet hem. The one thing she did not put on were the rings that had gotten her into so much trouble. They were safely in her safety deposit box. She'd put them there the morning after Mac left.

And there they would stay. Irrationally she

blamed the rings for getting her into this predicament. Since Connie wouldn't let her return them, they could do no damage in the box as they had done when she wore them.

The weather was warm and sunny and the outfit made her feel happy. She walked from her house toward Velma's. She wondered what Mac had told his friends about their engagement. Had he already told them it was broken? Technically, it was broken. It hadn't existed in the first place, but Cinnamon, again making logic irrational, felt as if they had somehow broken an engagement.

Pushing those thoughts aside, she entered Velma's with a ready smile. It died the moment her eyes connected with Mac's. He was sitting in the middle of the room with Allison and Paul. Allison saw her and waved her over.

"This was a mistake," she muttered to herself. Cinnamon looked around, hoping she could encroach upon someone else, but as usual, Velma's was packed. Fletcher sat with Amanda Sweeney at a table for two. Allison, Paul, and Mac sat at a table for four. There was one empty chair.

"It had to happen sometime," Cinnamon again muttered to herself. She wasn't going to be able to live in Indian Falls and not run into him. She may as well go through the test now.

Reluctantly, she threaded through the tables and walked directly up to Mac.

"Join us," Allison said.

"Yes," Paul agreed with her.

Mac stared at her. "We've just ordered, so you're in luck," he said. Apparently, he was testing her, too.

Cinnamon took a seat. Instantly a waitress appeared and took her order.

"I've been meaning to come by," Allison said, when the young woman left them. "But things have been a little hectic at our house."

Sheepishly she looked at Paul. He had ruddy-colored skin and it went a shade darker at her comment.

"Mac, I see you're back in town. I thought you left last weekend." Cinnamon's voice sounded formal and strained to her ears.

"I needed some things that were stored at Allison's. I'm officially moving to Washington."

The news hit Cinnamon like a lead bullet. She'd run him out of town. His association with her had caused him to uproot himself and move away from the town he loved.

"It's because of our marriage," Allison said with a smile. "Mac thinks we need the house alone."

"He's right," Cinnamon agreed, knowing Allison

was giving her an excuse. Cinnamon looked at Mac. His eyes were dark daggers.

The food arrived and for a moment everyone was quiet. Cinnamon didn't know how she could swallow with the lump in her throat. She drank some of her coffee to dislodge it.

"How was your trip?" Cinnamon asked. "I never got the chance to ask that night at your house." It was an opening, Cinnamon thought, a safe conversation, something to fill the airwaves while Cinnamon sat there with Mac so near. Allison chatted happily while they ate. Paul joined in occasionally, but Mac said nothing. It got her through the meal. When the waitress refilled their coffee cups, Allison and Paul refused another cup.

"We hate to eat and run, but we have an appointment at the photographer. Our photos are ready and I can hardly wait to see them," Allison said.

"Well—" Cinnamon began.

"No." Allison stopped her. "Stay and enjoy your coffee."

Cinnamon watched in dread as her chaperones left them. She and Mac were in a room packed with people, but they were alone.

"Mac," she began as soon as Paul wheeled Allison through the door. "I want to apologize for

last week. I know this started out as a joke, and you warned me more than once that it could go too far. I'm sorry. I never should have gotten you involved."

His features relaxed. He reached for his cup. "So are we back to being friends?"

Friendship was the last thing she wanted from him, but she nodded.

"Are you really moving up to Washington?"

"I can't stay with Allison and Paul and I have no room at Zahara's. It's better if I settle myself. I like Washington and, as you said, my house is a great place to live, not just work."

Cinnamon didn't like her words coming back to haunt her. She was going to miss Mac. She missed having him in the house, missed spending time with him. When he came to visit Allison, it was likely she wouldn't even know, unless she happened to run across him like she had this morning.

The place started to clear out and Cinnamon thought she should end the conversation and leave, too, but she was reluctant to do so. She wanted to be around Mac.

"Cinnamon, we saw the paper. Who is the guy?" Fletcher asked from a nearby table where he and Amanda were sitting.

"He's no one you know," she said.

"You know, he looks a lot like Mac," the young

waitress said. She looked at a newspaper on Fletcher's table as she poured him more coffee. "The eyes are the same and those dimples."

Cinnamon felt as if the joke was going to haunt her for the rest of her life. She glanced at Mac. His face was straight, but his eyes were dancing.

"The joke is over," Cinnamon said. "There is no man in my life."

Fletcher and Amanda came over. "Then where did the picture come from?"

"It was something that was done as a joke and somehow the papers got it. Can we forget that it was ever in the paper? There must be some other news they can find to fill space."

"You know what I think?" the waitress asked.

"What?" Amanda asked.

"I think you and Mac should get married." She gave them a wide smile as she swung her glance between the two of them. "The solution is so simple," she said. "I can't believe no one has thought of it before. Then you and Mac can live in the house together."

Fletcher Caton jumped on the idea. "Great solution," he said. "Zahara would approve of that. And it will give me a name to put on the invitation in place of Groom: TBA."

"What's this?" Connie Anderson walked over. "Who's the groom?"

"Mac here," Fletcher said.

"Wait a minute," Mac interjected. "I have not said I wanted to marry—" He stopped, looking at Cinnamon.

"Well, man, what are you waiting for? Go on and ask her," Connie prompted.

"Guys," Cinnamon started. "This isn't the right place. Mac and I need to talk."

"Haven't you talked enough?" Fletcher asked, then turned back to Mac. "Go on, Mac."

"Cinnamon, I—"

"Mac—"

They both began at the same time.

"Do you want to marry me?" Mac asked.

She could feel the tension in the four people hovering over them. She felt Mac was coiling as tightly as a spring. He hadn't exactly asked the right question. She was sure he didn't want her to say she did.

"Mac, I didn't come to Indian Falls looking for a husband."

"But, it's all right if you find one," the waitress said. "Go on, honey, answer his question."

Cinnamon looked into Mac's eyes. She was trying to find an answer there, hoping something

in the depths of those melting brown eyes would give her a clue. At first she thought she saw fear, but it gave way to something else. It looked like desire, but it could just as well be a signal for her to refuse.

She was confused. She remembered them making love. The way he made her feel when he touched her. The way she'd been so miserable this last week after he'd left. Her ears grew as hot as a sunspot. She wanted to recreate that night of love. She wanted Mac in her life.

"Yes," she breathed. Suddenly the room was applauding. Cinnamon snapped out of her dream world. She'd said yes, but she wasn't answering the question, not Mac's question. She was replying to her own memory of the nights that had changed her life.

She glanced at Mac. His eyes were wide and surprised.

"Mac, I didn't—"

"Mac, aren't you going to kiss her?" Fletcher interrupted her. "I swear young folks don't know how to be young."

Mac got up and moved to the seat next to her. He took her hand.

"Mac, I think we should talk about this," she whispered so only he could hear.

"It's too late," he told her.

"You don't really want to marry me. You told me so."

His hand came up and he pushed her hair back from her face. Then his mouth was on hers, and the love was back between them.

A great whooping sound brought Cinnamon back to her surroundings. The entire crowd was applauding and making noise.

"Set a date," Fletcher said. "I need something to put on the invitation."

"We can't set a date," Cinnamon said. "It takes time to plan a wedding."

"Everything's planned," Connie said.

"Yeah," Amanda agreed. "You've got a dress, the rings, the cake."

"I know Velma will cater," the waitress said.

"Mac, help me out here." Cinnamon appealed to him.

"How about the third Saturday in August?"

"That's not the answer I wanted."

"August twentieth." Fletcher seized the date. "That'll work." He slapped Mac on the back and headed for the door.

"Congratulations," the waitress said and returned to serving coffee. Everyone seemed to return to

their normal lives. Cinnamon's had been changed again.

And she had done it.

And Mac had helped. Did he really want to marry her?

"We have *got* to talk," she told him.

"How's it feel?" Mac asked. "It isn't so funny now."

"Mac, what are you talking about," she whispered. "You just let all these people think we're going to be married."

"Yes," he said. "I did."

Chapter 11

By morning Mac was gone. As far as Cinnamon could tell, he'd left the restaurant and returned to the District without a word. She didn't understand what was going on. She'd completely lost control of her life. This was a joke. What Mac had said was a joke. He was letting her know what it felt like to have things go wrong.

And she did know. But where was he? She needed to talk to him, especially after six boxes of wedding invitations arrived with Mac's name as groom printed in gold lettering on a creamy background. The bakery called to tell her she needed

to come in and choose a cake style. Even the minister called to congratulate her and tell her that August twentieth was available if she was planning to have the ceremony in Indian Falls.

Cinnamon refused to answer the phone again. The machine could pick up any further calls. And she had to get out of the house. Out of Indian Falls. Then she thought of Samara. Her sister could help her sort out this horrible predicament.

At that moment her cell phone rang. It was Samara. Cinnamon wondered how she knew that she needed her.

"Samara," she said, answering the call.

"I can't believe you're getting married and you didn't even tell your family. Have you talked to your mother? Have you even called Dad?"

"Stop, Samara."

Silence ended the tirade. "What's wrong?"

"Are you home?"

"Yes, I'm at home."

"Do you mind if I come up? I have got to get out of this town."

"Come on. We'll talk when you get here."

Cinnamon felt better by the time she pulled into a parking space in front of Samara's house and better still after she'd told her story and drunk two glasses of white wine.

Samara's house was much like Cinnamon's mother's. The walls and furniture sported bold colors. Her shades, however, were more muted instead of the screaming electricity that had surrounded Cinnamon daily.

"And he just sat there?" Samara laughed.

"Stop laughing," Cinnamon said, giggling herself. "This is not funny." Right after she said it, she burst into laughter.

"Well, what are you going to do?"

"I don't know." Cinnamon spread her hands. "I need to talk to him, but he seems to be gone."

"You know where he works and where he lives. You could go there."

"Samara, that's too melodramatic. This is not some movie."

"It's sure playing out like one." She laughed again.

"It was a publicity stunt to get some business for the merchants. It just got out of hand."

"Yeah!" she said. "And now there's a wedding date and three hundred engraved invitations with your names on them. I'd say that was a little out of hand."

"I can't imagine what the newspaper is going to print tomorrow."

"Or what your mother is going to say when she finds out."

Cinnamon sat straight up. The wine sloshed around in the glass, but did not spill. "Mother! She'll be livid that I didn't call her first thing."

"She'll probably arrive in Indian Falls with a tractor-trailer load of people and design the entire event, even if it is a hoax."

Cinnamon's mother was dramatic and both women knew it.

"She's something else to deal with. Right now you need to decide about Mac." Samara got her back on track.

"How can I decide when I haven't even talked to him?"

"That's what you need to decide, melodramatic or not."

"I could call the studio and ask for him."

"There is that. And if he's not there?"

"Samara, I am not going to his house unannounced."

"Why not? He came to yours unannounced. And spent the night. Several nights."

"It wasn't like that. He rented a room and you know it." The giggles were back.

"And what was his payment?"

Cinnamon and Mac agreed on a consideration.

It was not monetary. Maybe it should have been, she thought. But what they had as consideration was better than any currency on earth. Her ears burned hot at the thought of them in the bedroom Mac had used.

Samara got up. "I'm going to get some more wine. Here's the phone. You'll find the number in here."

Dropping the phone book on her lap, Samara went into the kitchen. Cinnamon opened the book and found the studio's main number. She was sure someone would answer the phone at the television station, but not sure if she could get through to him. She dialed the number and hung up before anyone answered.

What was she going to say? Maybe it was her fuzzy mind, but nothing came. She'd had so many questions yesterday at Velma's, but now she couldn't think of anything to open the conversation.

Yet she was determined. She dialed. The operator answered and Cinnamon asked to speak to him. Without another question, she was put through. However, he did not answer. A woman answered, saying, *Newsroom*. She asked for him again giving her name.

"I'm sorry, Ms. Scott, he isn't here at the moment. We don't expect him until sometime on Tuesday."

"Tuesday?"

"Yes. He's giving a lecture to some broadcasting students at Howard University on Monday."

"Thank you," Cinnamon said. "I'll try to reach him at home," she lied.

"May I say congratulations on your engagement. It was quite a surprise for us to discover that Mac had a fiancée."

Cinnamon didn't know the person she was talking to and even with the wine playing fuzz with her brain, she was unwilling to say anything more than thank you. She hung up as Samara returned.

"He's not there."

"Call him at home."

"I don't have a number."

Samara dropped a small note in her lap.

"What's this?"

"His number. While you were on the phone, I used my cell and called a fri…someone who knows him. And got the number."

Cinnamon remembered the man in the cafeteria who was with Mac the day she'd had lunch with Samara.

"Call him," Samara commanded.

Cinnamon lifted the phone receiver and dialed the number. The Georgetown house came into

view in her mind. She wondered which room Mac was in. Was he sitting before the fireplace or in the bedroom? Was he alone? There was really no engagement between them, not even an understanding. There could be someone else there. Maybe even Jerrilyn.

"Hello."

She recognized Mac's voice. He had a bedroom voice, not just a low and sexy one, although it was all of that. It also had a dark, enveloping quality like warm arms enfolding her, keeping her safe. It was everything a woman could dream of—strong, authoritative, yet sensitive and damn sexy. Cinnamon felt aroused and so far he hadn't even gotten past "hello."

She sat up and shook herself, trying to clear her head.

"Mac, it's Cinnamon. I need to talk to you."

"Can it wait until morning? I'll be in Indian Falls then."

"I'm not in Indian Falls."

"Where are you?"

"At my sister's house. She lives on the upper end of Sixteenth Street."

"Here? In D.C.?"

Cinnamon nodded. "Yes."

"Would you like to come here?"

"No," she said. "I mean, I can't. I can't drive."

"Is something wrong? Are you hurt?" She could hear the instant concern in his voice. "Has there been an accident?"

"Nothing like that. Too much wine."

"Oh, I see." She wasn't sure what she heard in his voice. "Would you like me to come and get you?"

Cinnamon wanted to jump at that. Her mind shouted yes, but she subdued it. She needed to be clearheaded when she talked to him. "Can we meet tomorrow?"

"I'm busy all day. How about dinner?"

"Dinner will be fine."

She gave him her cell number and they hung up.

Taking a drink of her wine, she said, "That didn't sound like two people who were in love. More like two people planning a divorce."

Samara resumed her seat. "Cinnamon," she said. Her tone had totally changed.

Cinnamon looked at her sister.

"Are you in love with Mac?"

No was on the tip of her tongue, but she knew it wasn't true. "I think so."

"You think?"

"I know. I've known it for weeks."

"Does he know?"

"No." She shook her head.

"Why?"

"He doesn't want to marry me, Samara. He asked me to accompany him to a wedding because we didn't like each other. I was a ruse for his ex-fiancée."

"But things changed. They changed for you. Maybe they did for him, too."

Cinnamon pondered that. Was that why Mac set a date? Had he changed his mind and he really *did* want to marry her? Maybe it was the wine, but she clutched on to that answer. It was the one she wanted. By morning, clearheaded, she would think differently, but tonight she wanted to bask in the warmth that her love was returned.

By morning Cinnamon's head was clearer and she'd convinced herself that it was the wine that had her believing Mac might be in love with her. Samara had left for work by the time Cinnamon got out of bed. Fixing herself a cup of coffee, she flipped through the *Washington Post*. It was good to see a paper that didn't have a story about her and her impending marriage on the front page.

She scanned the sales at the major department stores, checked out the food ads and what was on sale at the chain pharmacies in the area. Then she turned to a Metro section and saw Mac's face

staring at her. The story was about the famous broadcasting executive speaking at Howard University. The woman on the phone had mentioned him speaking there.

Cinnamon read the story. It told of Mac's rise from street reporter to hosting his own television program. She must have gotten the idea then, for Cinnamon was sitting in the back of the darkened auditorium when Mac came on stage.

She was going to meet him for dinner anyway. She might as well attend the lecture and they could decide then.

Cinnamon didn't think that many people would attend a lecture at five o'clock, but the place was packed. Mac looked great onstage. She smiled and her heart fluttered at seeing him. This was his element. He shone here.

She'd never seen him speaking before. She'd watched his show, seen him host the program, facilitate a discussion and keep control of a subject. But she didn't really know his history, how he got started in the business. Why he chose journalism. She realized he didn't know the answers to those questions about her, either. They really didn't know each other. But that didn't stop her from being in love with him.

By the time they got to the question and answer

portion, Cinnamon had learned that Mac initially wanted to be a doctor—which she'd known—but what she hadn't been aware of was his motive, his sister's disease. Allison had other ideas, though, and convinced him to do what he really loved instead of trying to save her. The crowd sighed at that, and Mac went on to explain that Allison was fine and had been married just a few weeks ago.

He chose journalism because he wanted to know the truth and wanted to report it.

He got questions about getting into the job market and how hard it was to start. Finally a young man rose near the front and asked, "How do you feel when you *become* the news, instead of reporting it?"

Cinnamon immediately knew where this was going. Mac frowned as if he didn't understand the question, but she knew he was too good a journalist to miss the point. He was buying time.

"No reporter wants to be the subject of a story, unless he wins the lottery." The audience laughed.

When the laughter died down, the young man stood again. "I mean the story about you and the weather girl from Boston."

Cinnamon held her breath.

"She's a meteorologist. She has a doctorate in her field and she's a young woman, not a girl," Mac explained.

Cinnamon breathed out.

The questions continued. The audience was composed of journalism majors. They appeared to have gone into reporter mode and were badgering Mac for answers to questions that would get at the truth. It was obvious Mac didn't like being on the hot seat.

"So, after all the stories that appeared in the *Indian Falls Weekly,* you're going to marry Dr. Scott?"

Cinnamon leaned forward. She was interested in the answer to this question.

"Dr. Scott and I had some discussion since that last story appeared and we decided to break our engagement."

Cinnamon gasped. In the quietness of the room, her reaction was audible. Mac looked in her direction. She dropped her head, but she was sure it was too dark for him to see her.

"Who broke the engagement?"

"It was mutual."

"So you're not in love with her?"

Questions were thrown at him from all points in the room. A rhythm had developed and Mac answered as fast as they were asked. On the last one, he held up his hands to stop them.

"These questions don't seem to have anything to do with journalism."

"Just for the record, *are* you in love with her?" came another question.

"I'm not in love with anyone. And I don't plan to marry. Ever."

Cinnamon felt as if he'd punched her in the stomach. If she hadn't been sitting six seats in, she'd have left. But she didn't want to make a spectacle of herself. She couldn't listen to anything else. Her mind whirled. Her stomach churned.

The applause snapped her back to reality. The lights came up as people rushed to the stage to talk to Mac. Cinnamon remained in her seat. She wanted the other people to leave before she got up. Since they knew about her and Mac's engagement, someone might recognize her. Checking that Mac was still behind groups of students, she got up and hooked her purse over her shoulder. With one final look, she headed for the door. Just before she got there, a female student stared at her.

"Aren't you—"

"No." Cinnamon cut her off. As she went around her, she glanced at the stage and looked straight into the eyes of MacKenzie Grier. Without a word she left the auditorium.

There was no need to meet him for dinner. When her cell phone rang later that night, Cinnamon

was nearly back to Indian Falls. She saw Mac's number on the small display and turned the unit off. She'd had her discussion with him. There was nothing else to say. No matter how she felt, he wasn't in love with her.

That couldn't have been her, Mac thought. He'd looked up in the audience when he heard a voice he thought he knew. Then he'd seen her going through the door. She looked at him, but it was dark and a long way from the stage. She couldn't have been there. But where was she? He'd been calling her for hours. They were supposed to have dinner and she'd stood him up.

Finally at midnight, his phone rang. He grabbed for it and automatically looked at the number. He didn't recognize it. Something could have happened to her and this was a stranger calling to let him know.

"Hello," he said.

"MacKenzie Grier?" the voice asked. It was someone who didn't know him.

"Yes."

"This is Samara Scott, Cinnamon's sister. We had lunch together a couple of months ago."

"Do you know where she is?"

"She isn't with you?" Her voice rose a little.

"She stood me up. I've been calling her cell phone for hours."

"She wasn't here when I got home from work. Usually she'll call me if I'm expecting her and she isn't coming back. But when she didn't answer her cell, I got scared. Do you think she went back to Indian Falls?"

Mac hadn't thought of that. Indian Falls wasn't that far away. "I haven't tried to call her there."

"Wait a minute, she stood you up. Why would she do that? She really wanted to talk to you."

Mac hesitated a moment. "I think she was at my lecture today."

"What lecture?"

Mac outlined what he believed happened.

"But you're not sure it was her?" Samara asked.

"Not entirely. But since she's not answering her phone and she never called to firm up our dinner plans, what else can I think?"

"I'm going to call the house and see if she's there."

"If she answers, don't tell her you've talked to me."

"Why not?"

"She heard something pretty awful this evening. I want to have a chance to explain."

"All right if you answer one question for me?"

Mac didn't wait for the question. He knew what

it was. "The answer is yes," he said. "I do love her. I don't think I can go on living without her in my life."

"That's the right answer," Samara said.

Mac listened. Although there was no sound, he knew Samara was using another phone to dial the house in Indian Falls.

"Cinnamon, thank God you're there. When you didn't call me, I got worried."

Mac didn't wait to hear anything else. He snapped his cell phone closed and left the house. Within minutes he was in his car and speeding out of the District. He made it to Indian Falls in record time. The lights were on in Zahara Lewis's house. Mac still had the keys Cinnamon had given him when he was renting the room. He didn't use them, but rang the doorbell. Cinnamon didn't answer immediately, but Mac knew she was there.

He rang the bell again, punching it to get her attention. Eventually, she opened the door.

"I want to talk to you," Mac said. He had a foot inside the threshold in case she tried to push him out.

Cinnamon looked down and walked away from the door. He'd expected her to be angry, to rant, scream or show some volatile reaction. She moved like he was any Sunday guest who'd dropped by for a visit.

"Would you like something to drink?" she asked.

"I saw you," he said, ignoring her offer.

"Where was that?" She smiled brightly, giving him an on-camera smile. "At the lecture hall?"

"Cinnamon, I can explain."

"What a cliché," she said. "Why do you think there is anything you need to explain? We're not engaged. We never have been. From the first, this was a joke. You didn't like it, but that's what it was. So, no hard feelings. You can go now."

"I love you," he said.

She stared at him. Her eyes narrowed and her voice was low and angry. "What did you say?"

"I said, 'I love you.'"

"Get out of here!" she shouted.

"That's not the reaction I expected."

"What did you expect? That it would mean something to me? That not seven hours ago you stood in front of a crowd of students and told them you were not in love with anyone and not likely to be, yet here you are saying 'I love you'? Well, I'm not buying it. Now I'd appreciate it if you'd leave."

This was not going well. Mac hadn't intended to blurt out that he was in love with her. But the words found their way to his mouth and they were out before he could think about it.

Cinnamon went to the door and opened it. She stood waiting for Mac. He shrugged, knowing there was nothing else he could do except leave.

Chapter 12

Sleep wasn't on the menu after Mac had walked out the door. Cinnamon was emotionally drained. Sitting down on the sofa, she tried to get her feelings back in line. Her mind replayed the scene with Mac.

He'd told her he loved her.

And she'd thrown him out.

What had happened to her since she came to Indian Falls? How could things go so wrong? Maybe she should have stayed in Boston. Maybe she should go back there. It was obvious all she'd caused since she set foot in Indian Falls was hardship and embarrassment. She understood Boston, knew the mechanics of it. Even if she didn't like her treatment there, no one cared if she was engaged to be married or just plain living with someone.

In Indian Falls, her life was front-page news.

The whole town was involved in her affair. Affair, she seized the word. She and Mac didn't have an affair. There was no word for what they had. *Nothing* wasn't correct and *something* was too strong a word to name what was between them. They did have *some*thing. Only she couldn't define it.

The chimes on the grandfather clock in the hall began to ring as they counted out the hour. Cinnamon listened. It was three o'clock in the morning. She should go to bed, but she knew she wouldn't sleep. Cinnamon got up and started for the kitchen when the doorbell rang again.

Stopping, she turned and looked at the door. It could only be Mac. Who else would ring her doorbell at this hour? For a split second, Cinnamon considered ignoring it, but what good would that do? He knew she was there. The lights were still on and there was that staccato punching of the doorbell that was nothing if not a signature of the man.

Going to the door, she yanked it open.

"I'm back," he said and pushed past her into the room.

Cinnamon closed the door, but stood where

she was. Her shoulders felt as if they had weights on them.

"Why are you here?"

"To talk some sense into you."

"Why do you think I'm the one who's out of my senses?"

"Because you're in love with me and I'm not leaving until you admit it."

"All right, I admit it. Go."

She started to open the door. Mac moved faster than she'd ever seen anyone move. He pushed the door closed and pinned her against it. His hands weren't touching her. No part of his body made contact with hers, yet Cinnamon was held in place as surely as if he'd stuck daggers through her clothes.

"Say it out loud." His voice was seductive. He put his forehead against hers. "Say it out loud," he teased. Cinnamon felt his breath brush her skin. It was as solid as if his hands were caressing her. Her body began a meltdown. She knew she wouldn't be able to hold on. "Say it, Cinnamon. I need to hear the words.

"I love you," she said.

In an instant his mouth was on hers. Mac's hands dug into her hair, holding her mouth still as he kissed her. His lips ravished hers, his tongue sweeping into her mouth and taking all that she gave. Cinnamon's entire body seemed to be part of the kiss. Arousal felt like small bubbles under her skin, each popping in an electric burst that infused her with a need greater than she'd ever experienced before.

She wanted Mac, wanted him more than she'd ever wanted anyone. She wanted a change to their status, to know that there was something definite keeping them together, making them part of the same whole. She wanted to spend her life learning about him, finding his secrets and keeping them safely locked in her heart.

Cinnamon's arms went around Mac and she held him tightly. She joined Mac in a kiss of desperation. She loved him. She'd told him so and he'd said as much. Her world had tilted. She was delirious, happy, rapturous.

Mac lifted his mouth briefly. When he settled it again on her, the kiss changed. The desperation that had been in them both was gone. He cradled her against him. His hands felt less insistent in her hair, yet they were soft and caring as they touched her. His mouth worshipped hers. The world could have stopped turning for all Cinnamon knew. They seemed to stay that way for a long time. Then Mac slipped his mouth from hers, but kept her cradled against him.

Cinnamon thought of their argument earlier. How she'd thrown him out and if he hadn't come back…but he did come back.

"Thank you," she whispered to herself and only realized she'd said it out loud when he answered.

"For what?"

"For coming back. For loving me. For changing my world."

"Is that all?" he said. "You're welcome."

The sun shone through the open windows. Cinnamon opened her eyes. Stretching like a satisfied cat, she turned over in the bed, wrapping herself in the covers. She couldn't believe it. She and Mac were getting married.

It must be nearly noon, but Cinnamon didn't care. She and Mac had spent the night together in blissful union. At least the part of the night still available. Unfortunately, he had to return to Washington.

He'd awakened her with his body, his hands moving over her already naked form like warm pads, his mouth planting kisses along her spine. She was nearly liquid by the time he turned her over and made mad morning-love to her.

Cinnamon stretched again and wondered how Mac was doing. She smiled, lounging against the sex-scented sheets. Pushing herself up, she began her getting dressed ritual. It was after a cup of coffee that the doorbell rang and she found Allison Mathis sitting there in her chair.

"Allison, come in."

"Congratulations!" She reached up, her arms outstretched. "Mac called me this morning. I couldn't be more pleased." Her smile was wide and genuine.

Cinnamon hugged her and then helped her inside.

"Want some coffee?"

"Love some."

The two went to the kitchen and several minutes later were seated at the table.

"So, we don't have much time," Allison began. "Mac should never have chosen a date so close. It took me a year to plan my wedding. But you have most of the details already done."

She ran on. Cinnamon listened, but said nothing.

"You have the invitations, the flowers, the church." Suddenly she stopped, putting her hand up to her mouth and then moving it. "Oh, I'm sorry. I haven't given you a moment to say anything. I'm just so excited. I never thought Mac would marry. Not after…"

"After Jerrilyn," Cinnamon finished for her. "I've met her. She's beautiful."

"But she was wrong for him."

"I know," Cinnamon cooed. Flashes of last night went through her mind.

"But you're right for him," Allison said, reassuring her.

"Thank you."

"Mac could hardly speak this morning. I've never seen him so excited. Now, what can I do to help?" Allison worked as the head of finance in a large car-dealership. She dealt with people all day. "I know I had Mac doing a lot of the legwork for me, but that was just to keep his mind occupied."

"Oh, no!" Cinnamon suddenly thought.

"What's wrong?" Allison's face was a mask of concern.

"I don't know if I can have a wedding."

"Why not?"

"I've got to tell my mother. And she'll freak."

"Why?"

"Let's just say it's probably a good thing that we have only a month to witness the war between the states."

The wedding began at exactly five o'clock. Cinnamon's mother had been seated in the front pew. All the bridesmaids had marched down the aisle on the arm of a groomsman and now it was her turn. Cinnamon looked at her father. She was surprised to see tears in his eyes.

He was a good-looking man with only a few gray hairs. Samara looked more like him than Cinnamon did, although he had clear skin the same color as hers. She'd gotten that from him.

"You're beautiful," he said, looking at her. Cinnamon looked down at herself. She wore Allison's wedding gown. It had arrived the day after Allison came to see her. Cinnamon hadn't been expecting anything, but in Indian Falls wedding gifts arrived at any time. She was surprised to find a deliveryman standing there with a large box. Opening it she found the wedding gown—Allison's wedding gown. There was a note. It read, "this is not the wrong wedding gown. It was meant to be yours."

"Wasn't it just yesterday that you were going to kindergarten?" Her father's voice snapped her back to the present.

Cinnamon pressed her cheek to his. "Yes," she acknowledged. "That was yesterday."

"Today, you're all grown up and a bride." He smiled. "Mac's a lucky guy," he said. "And I made sure he knows it."

Cinnamon took his arm as the doors were flung open. They looked down the long aisle and heard the notes of the wedding march.

"It's time," she said.

He kissed her cheek again. And they started.

Cinnamon looked for Mac. He stood at the front of the church. He smiled at her. The tension that had been on his face at the other weddings was gone. She floated toward him. From now on everything would be fine.

Book #2 in the Three Mrs. Fosters miniseries...

THE
PERFECT
MAN

National bestselling author

CARLA
FREDD

Renee Foster's genius IQ intimidates most men—
but not Chris Foster, her late husband's brother.
Chris seems the perfect man for Renee, except he refuses
to settle down...and Renee won't settle for less..

"*Fire and Ice* is a provocative romance that snaps, crackles and
sizzles into an explosive, unforgettable reading experience."
—*Romantic Times BOOKreviews*

Coming the first week of June wherever books are sold.

KIMANI
ROMANCE

The second title in the Stallion Brothers miniseries...

TAME A WILD STALLION

Favorite author

DEBORAH FLETCHER MELLO

Motorcycle-driving mogul Mark Stallion falls fast and hard
for gorgeous mechanic Michelle "Mitch" Coleman. But
Mitch isn't interested in a pretty, rich boy who plays with
women's hearts...despite the heat generated between them.

"Mello's intriguing story starts strong
and flows to a satisfying end."
—*Romantic Times BOOKreviews* on *Love in the Lineup*

Coming the first week of June wherever books are sold.

KIMANI™
ROMANCE

www.kimanipress.com

KPDFM0690608

Destined *to* MEET

Acclaimed author
devon vaughn archer

When homebody Courtney Hudson busts loose for one night, she winds up in bed with sexy Lloyd Vance, an Alaskan cop escaping a troubled past. Then tragedy strikes and they're caught in a twist of fate that threatens to destroy their burgeoning love.

"[*Christmas Heat*] has wonderful, well-written characters and a story that flows."
—*Romantic Times BOOKreviews*

Coming the first week of June wherever books are sold.

"*Obsession* is a five-star delight."
—Harriet Klausner, America On Line Reviewer Board

Essence bestselling author

GWYNNE FORSTER

Obsession

Turning her back on her career, Selena Sutton
settles in a small Texas town where she becomes
entangled in an explosive triangle of desire.
After fighting off the unwanted advances of spoiled
playboy Prince Cooper, she's courted by his brother
Magnus, whose tenderness takes her breath away.
Now the object of both brothers' obsession,
Selena learns the cost of unstoppable passion...
and how priceless true love can be.

*Coming the first week of June
wherever books are sold.*

ARABESQUE®

www.kimanipress.com   KPGFI030608

These women are about to discover that every passion has a price...and some secrets are impossible to keep.

NATIONAL BESTSELLING AUTHOR

Rochelle Alers

After Hours

A deliciously scandalous novel that brings together three very different women, united by the secret lives they lead. Adina, Sybil and Karla all lead seemingly charmed, luxurious lives, yet each also harbors a surprising secret that is about to spin out of control.

"Alers paints such vivid descriptions that when Jolene becomes the target of a murderer, you almost feel as though someone you know is in great danger."
—*Library Journal* on *No Compromise*

Coming the first week of March wherever books are sold.

sepia™

www.kimanipress.com

KPRA1220308